A JAR OF
FINGERS

THE COMPLICATED LIFE OF DEEGIE TIBBS BOOK 1

C. L. HERNANDEZ

A PERMUTED PRESS BOOK

ISBN: 978-1-68261-595-9

PERMUTED PRESS

Permuted Press, LLC
New York • Nashville
permutedpress.com

Published in the United States of America

For Olivia Marie, my greatest blessing

PROLOGUE

December, 1927

"SOME STRANGE THINGS WENT ON in that house, that's for sure," the old cop said as he spat on the rain-wet ground.

The two uniformed officers, one a rookie, one a hardened veteran, stood on the frosty lawn at 14 Fox Lane, smoking Luckys and watching the bodies of two dead brothers being trundled down the sidewalk on squeaky-wheeled gurneys.

"Looks like they both took some kinda poison, from what the coroner says. Faces all black and swollen, green foam comin' outta their mouths, sure sign of poison they say," the older cop said, and he flicked his cigarette butt into a puddle of rainwater and turned to gauge the rookie's reaction. The kid's face was grim and pale, but so far he hadn't puked.

"I know," the rookie muttered. "I saw." He puffed on his cigarette without inhaling.

"I'm thinkin' we got ourselves a double suicide." The older cop hitched up his belt and scratched thoughtfully at his stubbled chin. "Guess the boys downtown will figure that out for us though, huh?" He waved a hand under his nose, wafting away an imaginary stink cloud. "Shoo! I can still smell 'em, can't you? Been layin' dead in there for at least a week, I'd say." He glanced at the kid again, and observed with no surprise that his face had gone even paler. "Hey kid, you alright?"

"Sure." The rookie nodded and turned away. "'Scuze me a sec."

He headed for the side of the house, walking swiftly. Faint retching sounds followed.

"He'll get used to it after a while," said the older cop to no one in particular.

The double suicide at 14 Fox Lane was the main topic of conversation in Fiddlehead Creek, Washington for more than a week. The local newspaper featured a different lurid photograph of the tragic scene every day: the house itself, with the two policemen standing to the side; the coroner, leaning over the blanket-draped deceased and staring grimly into the camera; and a shot of the two brothers as they were in life, grinning and holding a stringer of trout between them.

Everyone had their own opinion of what had actually happened in the living room of that old house. Some claimed the brothers were terminally ill, and took their own lives to avoid prolonged suffering. Others thought that the deaths hadn't been suicides at all and the brothers' murderer was still lurking in the woods on the edge of town. Then there were the ones who claimed to have been there when the detectives had taken out box after box of mysterious items: paintings of demons, books written in strange languages, and dozens of skulls and bones from small animals. "It was devil worship!" they claimed in hushed voices, and a few of the locals took to walking on the other side of the street when passing by the house at 14 Fox Lane. Children made up stories about the ghosts they had seen peering out of the upper story windows, and a wandering vagrant once ran screaming into the local jail house, demanding to be locked up because the ghosts of the dead brothers were chasing him.

Eventually, as with all small-town scandals, the excitement died down, and people got on with their lives. The house at 14 Fox Lane was bought and sold several times, but no one really wanted to live there. It sat empty on its spacious lot, growing faded and splintery in the summer sun and winter snows while the Umatilla National Forest slowly reclaimed the property. Brambles and weeds took over the backyard, and the rose bushes grew wild, unpruned and uncared for. Pine needles sifted down through the lofty branches of the trees and formed a thick mat over the once well-tended back lawn. It was as if Nature herself wanted to conceal the secret that lay hidden there. Inside, the air grew stale and musty. Dust balls tumbled lazily across the once gleaming hardwood floors, trundled along by the drafts that found their way in.

Deep in the bowels of the house, veiled in darkness and the dust of decades, something slumbered, fitful and angry, waiting for the day when it would be set free.

CHAPTER ONE

DEEGIE SAT ALONE AT THE ornate iron table. Her hands basked in the warmth of the extra-large, extravagantly priced cup of coffee she held, but the dainty iron chair was freezing so she stood up and glanced up and down the sidewalk, trying to look as casual as possible. She always felt edgy at the end of the month; the delivery man was so damn creepy. He wore a navy blue beanie, no matter what the season, and had piggy little eyes that squinted and blinked spastically.

And he always found her, no matter where she was.

She heard him before she saw him; he wore hobnail boots which made a singular clickety-clack on the chilly Washington sidewalk. He rounded the corner of the donut shop, a squinting mole of a man bundled in a too large overcoat. To herself, Deegie called him Moley, but his real name was Mr. Hack, which reminded her of phlegm.

"Miss Tibbs," Moley dipped forward at the waist in a brief bow and handed her a thick manila envelope which she folded over and tucked into her purse.

The ritual had been the same for the past eleven years, beginning the night she lost her parents.

"You are in a different place now, a different city," Moley said, showing a scattering of teeth. "Still with the same man?"

"Yes. And no, he doesn't know, don't worry." Deegie answered his next question before he could ask it. Moley never seemed to trust her; he had the same set of questions every time. She would never tell Spencer, her boyfriend, that she received an envelope stuffed full of cash every month from a shady little man who looked like a garden pest. Spencer hardly paid her any attention anyway. He didn't even know she was a natural-born witch, not that she'd tell him that either.

"There are those who would harm you if they knew. No one must know." He glowered at her suspiciously between blinks.

"Yes, Mr. Hack, I know. I'll be careful. See you next time."

"No matter where you are." Moley offered his standard parting quote, then clickety-clacked back down the sidewalk. The ritual was complete; her monthly inheritance payment was delivered.

Deegie slid her hand inside her purse and felt the envelope. It was thicker than usual, which sometimes happened, and she smiled to herself. Her secret stash was building up. She hurried back to her vehicle and sat inside, sipping coffee and counting the thick stack of hundreds in the envelope. Combined with her savings, she had more than enough money for her own place. Today might just be the day. The money felt strangely warm, as it always did. Deegie had long suspected that Moley came from somewhere far south of here. Her father had been a dark witch, after all; he was bound to have had Underworld connections at some point in his life. *Perhaps that's where he is now*, she thought.

Thanks, Mom and Dad. Love you. In her mind, she colored the thought form a golden pink, added sparkles and red and pink hearts, then sent it bursting out into the Universe. She knew it would reach them.

It was funny how things worked out for Deegie.

She drove back to the A-frame house she shared with Spencer Pratt, her on-and-off boyfriend of three years. His car was in the driveway, the first sign that something was wrong. After making sure that her bulging purse was securely zipped, she hurried, frowning, to the front door. Spencer never came home early, never stayed home sick. Trying to stifle the alarm bells going off in her head, she went into the house. It was dim inside; not a light was on.

She heard music coming from behind their closed bedroom door, and she hurried in that direction.

"Spencer?"

The music stopped abruptly, and she heard a shuffle, a thump, and hushed, frantic voices. She opened the door, and her heart plunged all the way down to the floor.

"Oh. I see. You son of a *bitch!*"

Spencer stood poised on one leg, fighting for balance as he struggled into his boxers, and the peroxide blonde from next door cowered in the bed and covered her silicone breasts.

"Deegie! I didn't know you were—I mean, I thought you worked—"

"Nope." Deegie's lips tightened into a grim line, and she slammed her purse down on the dresser. "And you told me you were working today. Looks like you got your days mixed up."

The blonde reached for her clothes that lay scattered across the carpet, but Deegie toed them out of the way. "Oh no. You stay right there," she said. "I have a little surprise for you two love birds."

She backed away and stood blocking the doorway, arms across her chest. Yep, today was definitely the day. The extra money had been a sign. She balled her hands into tight, vibrating fists, let the outrage and hurt rise and boil, and then released it in the most effective way she knew.

* * *

Across from the tidy little A-frame on High Street, an old man woke up in the tool shed of a vacant rental home. Loud voices had disturbed his nap, and his head still pounded from all the two-for-one gin and tonics he'd had to drink last night. *Damn young couple must be fightin' again,* he thought with a grimace. He opened the door to the tool shed, poked his head out and took a cautious look around, then stepped out into autumn chill and golden sunlight.

Guess I'll find my truck and head on home. He wasn't quite sure how he'd wound up all the way over here on High Street, but this certainly wasn't the first time this had happened.

"Femina ad rana!" a woman's voice shouted from across the street, and a garish burst of colored lights, green, red, and brilliant gold, lit up the windows of the A-frame.

The old drunk's hands flew to his face to cover his still-bleary eyes. *"What the Sam Hill is that?"*

A flock of birds, spooked by the flash of light and the old man's strangled cry, flew in a squawking, flapping cloud to the next lot. The drunk peered through his stubby fingers and wondered if his hangover was worse than he'd thought. The stale alcohol in his belly burbled and rose sluggishly, and he wondered if he was going to vomit. Maybe this was that alcoholic hallucin-whatsis the doctor was always going on about, or the delirium tremens, or something.

"Imgens vir uber!" the woman cried, and a series of loud pops followed, each accompanied by its own impossibly bright color.

"Yup, yup, I'm a sick one today, I'm a sick one." The old drunk turned around and headed back to the tool shed, mumbling to himself and swiping at his filmy eyes. "Just a bit more shut-eye. Yup, that'll fix things." He wrenched the aluminum door shut and found the piece of tarp he'd wrapped around himself last night.

"Amittere memoria!"

The woman's angry scream was muffled by the flimsy metal shed, and the old drunk was glad he couldn't see the flashes of light this time. "No more gin," he muttered with his hands over his ears. "No more gin. That's what did it, yup. From here on out, it's nothin' but beer."

* * *

Deegie Tibbs tucked her house key into her officially dumped boyfriend's loosely curled hand and hauled the strap of her tightly packed duffle bag over her shoulder. "Well, I guess that's it then," she said with honest regret. She got no reply and wasn't expecting one. Spencer was still snared in her Chill Out Spell, and he wouldn't be saying much for another couple of hours. He sprawled languidly on his seventies-era couch and watched her with glazed and dreamy eyes. His fingers twitched as he tried to fold them around the key, and Deegie smirked at the goofy look on his face. "You'll come around in a few hours, asshole," she said.

Spencer was so damn sensitive; he'd be bawling like a kindergartner if it weren't for the Chill Out Spell. Although he was the one who had cheated and ultimately destroyed their relationship, she didn't want to risk causing him a panic attack while she left his sorry ass. Besides, he would have enough to deal with when he came out of his blissful state. She glanced at his chest with a wicked grin and resisted the urge to press a glossy red lip print onto his cheek.

She went to the roll top desk in the corner where a tiny purple frog splashed and flailed in a water-filled mayonnaise jar. "As for you, Danielle, you're going to have to get used to your new body." Deegie picked up the jar and peered at the little creature inside. Its dainty white throat pulsed with a frantic beat, and its froggy eyes bulged comically. The rims of its eyes still bore traces of bright green eye shadow and black liner. Soon that would fade, along with the bright purple of what was once a spandex yoga outfit, and the erstwhile Danielle Coltyn, yoga instructor, next-door neighbor, and boyfriend stealer would be an ordinary little yard frog trapped in a jar. Deegie tapped a black-lacquered nail against the jar; Danielle uttered a strangled croak and churned her webbed feet in the water.

"By the way, it's true," Deegie said, and she narrowed her striking blue eyes. "Witches really *can* turn people into frogs, have you noticed?" She tossed the jar into the air, giggled as it missed the ceiling by inches, then caught it and returned it to the desk. "You'll be amphibious and craving flies for oh, say three or four days. Then you'll return to your usual slutty, overly made-up self. You might want to be careful when that jar breaks, though.

Wouldn't want to get a nasty cut, would we?" She blew a kiss to the unfortunate creature in its glass prison. "Oh, there's just one more thing, D. Better hope Spencer doesn't find you before you change back into a hooker. He hates to see innocent creatures trapped in jars. He might decide to set you free in Orchard Park, and, well... let's just say there are a lot of hungry ducks waddling around out there."

She tipped a wave to the drooling mess lolling all over the couch. "Bye, Spence. Thanks for the memories, and enjoy your new breasts."

Spencer's t-shirt strained over his DDD chest, and he managed to roll his head in Deegie's direction. "Nughh..." he said.

It wasn't until Deegie got behind the wheel of her vintage Volkswagen Bus that she allowed herself the luxury of a few tears. She was, after all, human, albeit with extraordinary abilities. *Thank all the gods you didn't marry him,* she reminded herself as she started the Volkswagen's engine. The elderly vehicle shuddered as it came to life. A familiar pain wrapped itself around the back of Deegie's head and neck. She'd overextended herself again, and that pain was a warning that she'd better find a place to lie down before a full-blown migraine paid her a visit. She beeped the horn at Spencer's house just for the hell of it and drove to the spotless alleyway behind the magical supply shop she owned, The Silent Cat. Once securely parked, she fished around in her purse for her bottle of pain relievers, then went to the cot in the back of the Bus to lie down. The little spells she'd performed hadn't been big ones by any means, but for Deegie every spell came with a painful price.

A low bass rumbling rose from under the cot, and the cramped quarters filled with the scents of damp earth and the sun-warmed pelt of a large animal. Deegie's hand swept the empty space in front of her until her fingers sunk deep into coarse, familiar fur. "Tiger Spirit..." She smiled despite her distress, and opened her eyes. There was nothing to see but an angular slice of sunlight peering through a gap in the window curtain, but the young witch knew her guardian was there just the same. She felt his oily coat, heard his soothing rumble, and was ever so grateful for the comfort he brought.

"I'm okay," she said to the unseen feline spirit. "Just a little tired. It's not too bad this time, but thank you.

"Oh, and just in case you were watching me back there, I was only kidding about the ducks. There are no ducks in Orchard Park. I only said that to scare Danielle." Deegie felt her distress trickle away as she buried her face in Tiger Spirit's ethereal neck, and she managed a soft chuckle. "I can't say Spencer won't take pity on that little frog in a jar, though. He'll probably set her free in the backyard." She laughed now, despite the weakness in her limbs and the dull throbbing behind her eyes. "If he can stop screaming over his boobs long enough, that is."

Tiger rumbled, louder now, and she had a feeling he was scolding her. After all, it was against the Witch's Creed to alter another human's appearance. But the spells Deegie had used were basically harmless pranks, taught to her in secret by her father many years ago. Her mother would have been appalled, but her father, for all his faults, had had a wonderful sense of humor.

"They will both be fine in a few days, I promise. I was just mad, that's all. And yes, I remembered to use the Forget Me Spell, so they won't remember me." (The spell's real title was long and difficult to pronounce; Deegie had made her own adjustments.)

A soft growl, trailing up at the end in a rough-edged musical note.

"And yes, I'm sorry. I overreacted."

It wasn't that she actually understood the guardian spirit's grunts and rumbles. Since she was a little girl, she'd always made up the things that Tiger might tell her on his visits. She'd spent many long hours playing in her room having long conversations with the voice she provided for Tiger, pouring him make-believe tea from a pink plastic teapot. Later, when she became a teenager, Deegie would snuggle close to Tiger's huge, spirit form body and whisper to him of all matters that a teen girl found important: prom dates, and secret crushes, and whether she should try out for cheerleading. Although he never spoke, Tiger always listened.

The hot draft of clammy feline breath washed over her cheeks again and she felt the whack of a long tail against her leg, then the fading rumble of her guardian as he returned to the spirit world.

Deegie stayed where she was, parked in the alleyway behind The Silent Cat, and just before nightfall, when the sky slipped on its robes of purple and black, she felt well enough to unlock the back door of her shop and brew a pot of herbal tea on the hotplate behind the counter. Having lived in the Bus before on two other occasions, she wasn't particularly worried about not having an actual home—at least not for a few days. The Bus was older than she was, but the engine ran like a champ, and she'd turned the back part into a tiny, but fully livable, camper. It was early fall, and the weather was still warm, and she liked the idea of being close to The Silent Cat; she'd be fine here until she found a place of her own.

It will be an adventure, she thought as she inhaled fragrant steam. A brand new page in a brand new CHAPTER and all that jazz. And who the hell needs men anyway?

While the tea brewed, Deegie filled a one-ounce bottle of amber glass with drops of essential oils: rose oil blend, for stress and grief; lavender oil, for her headache; and clary sage, for depression and insomnia. She swirled the mixture clockwise and inhaled the magical scent as she envisioned her unhappy heart surrounded by a warm pink cloud that sparkled with flecks of gold. She filled the rest of the bottle with jojoba oil and added an eyedropper cap. This would be her daily fragrance until she got over the cheating asshat she'd once called her boyfriend.

CHAPTER TWO

THE SILENT CAT WAS A kaleidoscope of jewel tones against black. Packaged incense, in sticks and cones, hung on a pegboard by the register and exuded their combined aromas into a thick veil of scent which clung to hair and clothing and evoked thoughts of faraway lands and exotic places. An entire wall of Deegie's hand-poured candles, in dozens of shapes and sizes, stood out in a rainbow of deep greens, sultry blues, regal purples, and brilliant, blood-like reds. Gilt framed prints of gods and goddesses from various beliefs and religions hung in charming disarray on the black-painted walls, along with tie-dyed scarves, sarongs, and shawls. On the wall behind the register were row upon row of shelves filled with odd-smelling herbs and unusual potions. A glass display case contained essential oils in tiny bottles of brown or deep blue glass, while the top of the counter held baskets of herbal soaps, sage wands, and gemstone nuggets.

The building itself was old and drafty, but was surrounded by tall pines, and the great multi-paned bay window in the front made an ideal reading nook with the addition of a few mismatched chairs and end tables. Deegie offered her customers free herbal tea and a place to relax as they pored over her generous selection of books on witchcraft, aromatherapy, gem and mineral magic, and story collections full of myths and monsters. A small room in the back held overstock and wonders only Deegie knew about. It was blocked off with a black velvet curtain, a burgundy velvet rope suspended by two gold hooks, and a hand-lettered sign that read UNATTENDED CHILDREN WILL BE TURNED INTO FROGS.

Deegie entered through the back door, turned off the alarm before it could shriek, and made herself slap-dash presentable at the cracked and dripping sink in the shop's closet-sized bathroom. Not feeling up to her usual daily battle with her curly black hair, she tied it back into a loose pony tail and added a purple silk scarf. Her long neglected but fully paid for gym membership would come in handy now; she would need a place to shower. She circled her eyes with careless swipes of peacock-hued eye shadow and tried not to look at the rust stains on the porcelain while she scrubbed her teeth.

As she filled the register with the bag from the safe, she heard the whisper of tires against asphalt and went to the bay window to peer out at the parking lot. Spencer's rusty silver Nissan idled in the first slot in front of the door for a second longer, then he shut off the engine and unfolded his long body from the car.

Although she had effectively used the Forget Me Spell and Spencer would have no memory of their time together if he saw her, Deegie stifled a gasp and pulled back; this was the last thing she expected to see. She watched as he hesitated in front of the door, reading the shop's hours on the sign in the window, and holding his sweatshirt bunched over his pin-up girl chest. She'd never created a remedy for the Big Ol' Boobs Spell, and she wouldn't sell him one if she had, but it amused her to no end that he would go to the town's only magical supply shop for a cure instead of the emergency room of the local hospital. *What is he thinking?* she wondered. If she let him in, was he actually going to explain his situation to her?

"Hello, I woke up with a pair of gigantic knockers on my chest, and someone turned my side bitch into a frog. I'm too embarrassed to go to the hospital. Can you recommend a spell?"

Deegie pictured him saying those very words, then clapped both hands over her mouth and pressed down hard to keep the peals of laughter from tumbling out. It was funny how quickly a tragedy could turn into a comedy, but she almost felt bad for what she had done. Almost.

Just as Spencer raised his fist to knock on the door, another car pulled into the lot, a dusty blue Jeep with a faded Greenpeace flag tied to the antenna, and he turned and dashed back to his car with his enviable rack bouncing and his thick-framed glasses sliding down his nose. The Nissan's tires shrieked against the pavement as Spencer made a quick getaway.

Zach Altman got out of his Jeep and frowned at the odd scene he'd just witnessed. He went to the still-locked front door of The Silent Cat and checked his watch, noting that it was almost ten minutes past the shop's opening time. He didn't see Deegie's rainbow-painted hippie van in the lot. A bundle of newspapers tied with yellow plastic strips sat on the sidewalk next to the entrance. He rapped his thick knuckles against the door, and the pulled-down shade twitched a little. "Deegie? Deeg? You in there? You okay?"

From the other side of the door: "Yeah, hang on one sec. I'm late this morning!"

The lock snapped back, the glass paneled door rattled, and there stood Deegie Tibbs in all her rumpled glory. Her black lace skirt and Aerosmith T-shirt ensemble looked slept in, and her feet were swaddled in pink bunny slippers. A blob of toothpaste decorated the side of her mouth.

"Uh, Deeg?" Zach frowned. "You look like you slept in the car. Are you okay?"

She nodded and pointed at the bundle of newspapers. "Could you...?"

He picked up the bundle and she stepped aside to let him in. "What was up with that guy just now? Did he try something stupid with you or something?"

Deegie had to grin, but wisely kept the truth to herself. "Just some weirdo, I guess."

A good enough explanation; her customers knew nothing about her personal life, and she hadn't lived in Fiddlehead Creek long enough to form any real friendships yet. Her secret about Spencer and the sleazy neighbor chick would be safe enough. Moving all the way up here from California was turning out to be a good idea; business was certainly better, and the people were a lot less fake. Best to wipe the slate clean before it got too smudged.

"Yeah, there are a few around here," Zach said, and he pointed to the green velvet wing-backed chair by the window. "Can I—"

"Oh gosh. Yes, of course, go ahead," Deegie made fussing motions at her skirt and T-shirt, and switched on the hotplate under the teakettle. "I'm sorry," she smiled lamely, "I'm a bit of a spazz this morning. I'll have hot water for tea in just a sec, and—" she cut the plastic strip on the newspapers and handed him a copy "—here ya go. No charge today."

"Thanks." Zach still frowned as he sat.

Deegie set a well-scrubbed teacup and a basket of herbal teabags on the table in front of him, and when he glanced down at her hands, he figured things out for himself: the garnet ring she usually wore on her left hand was missing. She'd never mentioned a husband or boyfriend, and Zach had always been too shy to ask, but it made sense.

He patted her naked hand, then pointed in the general direction of her face. "You have a little...something...by your mouth, and, well, you're a little..." Zach stood up, put his hands on Deegie's shoulders, and steered her in the direction of the tiny bathroom. "Go on ahead, Deeg. Have a do-over. I'll keep an eye on things for you for a few minutes."

She nodded again, attempted a smile of thanks. She turned to close the bathroom door behind her, hoping he wouldn't see the tears on her cheeks.

She emerged a few minutes later, a few rough edges smoothed off, but still far from her usual self.

"Much better," Zach said. "Now fix yourself a cup of tea and come talk to me."

"Oh, I'm fine, really," Deegie poured hot water into a cup and sat down across from her faithful customer. "I just left my cheating ass of a boyfriend, that's all. I'll recover." She dipped a teabag in and out of her cup and blew a cloud of chamomile-scented steam across the table. The urge to tell him the rest of the story, the part about the revenge spells, was almost painful, but she forced it down and focused on her tea cup. Only Deegie's immediate family knew of her extraordinary gift, and most of them were dead.

"Sorry to hear that, Deeg. He's a moron, and a loser, and he doesn't deserve you, and all that other stuff I'm supposed to be saying."

Deegie picked up a plastic honey bottle in the shape of a bear and squeezed a golden glob into her teacup. "Gee, thanks, smart ass." She flicked a teabag wrapper at him and managed a real smile despite the tears in her eyes.

"Seriously though, Deeg. Sorry. His loss, I'm sure." Zach gave her hand a clumsy pat and scanned the parking lot again. Crying women made him nervous. "Where's your magic bus? He didn't take it, did he?"

"No. I parked in the back and slept there last night. No big deal."

"So you're homeless now? Is that what you're telling me? Deegie, I have a guest room you can—"

"I'm not homeless. I have everything I need in the Bus. I'll be fine there for now. I'm grateful for your offer, but I don't do the roommate thing very well, I'm afraid." She sipped her overly sweetened tea and made a face. "Besides, I'm going to look for a place soon. I've seen some great old houses around here. Maybe one of those. I've always wanted to buy a fixer-upper. Been saving for it, actually." She smirked bitterly as she thought of Spencer's ugly furniture and his complete lack of color-coordinating ability. "And now I can decorate my own place any way I want."

"There's a couple of old places on Fox Lane, but they're in bad shape." Zach raised a skeptical brow, his ginger beard gleaming in the sunlight pouring through the bay window. "Why would you want to live in an old beaten down place like that?"

"Because old houses have the best personalities." A car pulled into the lot, followed by another. Deegie smeared scarlet gloss on her lips and stood up. "Here come the troops," she said. "Hope it's busy as hell today. Work is the best thing for heartbreak."

"Is it?"

"I dunno. I just made that up."

The door banged open, and three black-clad teenagers with identical blue-black hair and solemn, downtrodden expressions filed into the shop. "It's emo time," Deegie whispered to Zach with a wink. "Gotta go."

She went to her stool behind the counter and held court over the magically inclined, the wanna-bes, and the simply curious. She answered the usual questions—some legitimate, some ridiculous. (Do voodoo dolls work? Is the magic on *Charmed* the real deal? Is that *real* graveyard dirt in that bottle?) She sold strong-smelling herbs and resins in folded paper bags, and wrapped newly purchased candles, mostly black, in layers of newspaper and bubble wrap. When the usual morning rush was over, and she looked up again, Zach had gone, leaving only his empty teacup and his business card from Altman Heating and Air. Deegie went to the table and picked it up. A sentence was scrawled across the back in blue ink: *I mean it. Call me. No strings attached.*

Deegie slipped the card in her skirt pocket, just in case.

* * *

After three days of roughing it in the back of the Bus, Deegie came to the conclusion that perhaps the gypsy lifestyle wasn't for her after all. Her back ached from the thin mattress, and having to leave the Bus and scurry to the shop at night so she could use the broom-closet bathroom got old quickly.

It didn't take her long to find what she was looking for. The average house hunter would most likely dismiss the old place at the end of Fox Lane as little more than a pile of old boards. Deegie saw a blank canvas, something to renovate and make beautiful. A "For Sale" sign hung by one nail on a post in the front yard, and had clearly been there for several years. Although the wind had made it ragged and the sun had faded its colors, the number scrawled across the bottom in black marker was still legible, and Deegie had called the realtor's office the next day. She'd found it slightly odd that the agent hadn't accompanied her, and even odder still when the response to her question had been a rather strident *Oh! THAT house?* Maybe they didn't like giving tours of the older houses; maybe they were afraid they'd get dust on their smart yellow blazers, or maybe they were allergic to cobwebs. It didn't matter to Deegie; she preferred going alone anyway. It was easier to feel the energy of a building without the static from other people.

Armed with a key to the front door, she stood in front of the house, looking up at the topmost windows and hoping she'd made the right decision to buy this place. It had obviously been lovely at one time. There were two main stories, a spacious attic, and a cellar. The front yard, once cleared of weeds and brambles, had plenty of room for flower beds and decorative statuary. It was in desperate need of paint and perhaps some minor repairs to the roof, yet, despite looking derelict, the house was still structurally sound and could easily stand for another hundred years. All it needed was a little love, care, and tending to.

The backyard was even bigger than the front, and the property line extended far into the wooded hill behind the house. She stood in dappled sunlight and surveyed what was once a large rose garden, judging by the snarls of dried, prickly branches and sickly leaves. The rusted remains of a garden bench protruded from the thicket of dead and dying rosebushes, and a thick tangle of wild blackberry bushes were slowly claiming their corner of the yard. It was too late for the berries; they hung, gently rotting, amid the wilted leaves.

But I could make pies next summer, she thought, *and jam, and smoothies, and blackberry hair rinse.*

A cracked and tilting bird bath leaned against what was left of a low stone fence; it was grimy and long neglected, but appeared to be carved from pink marble. Winged cherubs and clusters of grapes graced the pedestal. Definitely something that could be salvaged and restored to its former beauty. There was more than enough room for the greenhouse she'd always wanted, and visions of fresh herbs and homegrown tomatoes made her smile. Best of all was the wide back porch. Once it was cleaned, sanded, and painted, it could be enclosed with wire mesh and turned into a sun room for the cat sanctuary she'd always wanted to open. There was plenty of room on the old-fashioned porch for herself, too, and she could easily see herself lounging there, perhaps in one of those Adirondack chairs she'd been wanting.

Excitement rose buzzing and tingling inside her as she went around to the front of the house again and unlocked the door with the key the realtor had provided. She hadn't even seen the inside yet, and already she thought the place was perfect. Once she let herself in, she found that she was standing in the middle of the wide living room, in a patch of late afternoon sunlight which lay listlessly on the hardwood floor. Deegie felt spirit energy here, and to her this was a huge bonus; she was not afraid of ghosts, and she had had several supernatural experiences in her life. The presence was light and benevolent, and she couldn't help greeting it out loud.

"Hello? Anyone here?" She got no response, however. Perhaps what she'd felt had only been a figment of her hopeful imagination. It happened sometimes, even to highly sensitive individuals like

Deegie. She stepped into the long hallway which bisected the house and led to the kitchen. "Hey! You can talk to me."

At first her only response was the creaking of the old boards under her feet, then she definitely felt something: the skin on her arms tightened into goose bumps, and her scalp prickled, always a sure sign of a presence. She felt it watching her, felt its hesitancy, knew it had been far too long since it had been in contact with a human. It followed her into the kitchen, then hovered by the doorway, making a cold spot there.

"What a nice kitchen this is." She kept her voice gentle and her movements unhurried lest she frighten her new friend away, and she found herself thinking that a ghost would be the perfect housemate. Spencer had been such a slob; Deegie had spent countless hours picking up after him. Living with a ghost would provide a sense of companionship, but none of the mess. Just to the left of the kitchen at the end of the hall was a closed door with rusty hinges and a brown porcelain knob, most likely the door to a pantry or linen closet, and when Deegie tried to open it, she found it locked. *A mystery to be explored later,* she thought, and continued to view the house with her ghostly tour guide. Other equally old-fashioned doors on the first floor opened easily enough, and Deegie found three bedrooms, two large closets, and a small bathroom with a claw-footed tub.

To the right of the living room, a long flight of stars stretched up to the second floor, and they creaked indignantly as Deegie ascended them. She was likely the first person to be on those stairs in decades. The unseen presence followed. Once she had gained the second floor, she noticed the sudden swirling of sunlit dust motes just ahead of her, as if the spirit was now leading the way.

"It's very nice up here," Deegie said in a gentle voice. "Was your room up here, or did you have one of the big rooms downstairs?"

There was no reply, but she went on with her exploration of the second floor, chatting to the spirit who accompanied her as she roamed around. She sensed it listening, observing her every move, but she was far from perturbed; the spirits of the dead had always been attracted to her. To Deegie, it was as natural as breathing. After she'd finished her exploration of the second floor, she went back downstairs, trailing her hand along the dusty bannister. The curious spirit matched her step for step.

"Alrighty, then," Deegie went on, "I'm gonna go now. Just to let you know, though, I'll most likely be moving into this house, so just mind your manners." As she turned around and headed for the front door, she caught sight of something greyish and wispy, like an errant banner of smoke. It drifted in from the long hallway, molded itself into an almost human shape, and Deegie heard a feather-soft, whispered *"Don't...go..."* before the entity dissolved into nothingness.

"I'll be back," she promised out loud, and she turned to go for now, the key to her new home in her pocket.

CHAPTER THREE

DEEGIE FELT MORE AGITATED AMONGST the realty staff later that day as papers were signed and her savings account took an alarming dip. Her feet, clad in battered Doc Marten boots, took turns thumping out a bored rhythm on the level loop carpet as she deflected the cloud of nervous energy generated by everyone in the building. The fake smiles of the redhead manning the phone were annoying too.

"By the way," Deegie said as she helped herself to another cup of complimentary coffee, "I know the place is haunted, so don't worry. I'm not going to try to back out of anything, or demand my money back if ghosts come up through the toilets, or if I dig up a human skull in the basement, or anything of that nature." She added powdered cream and stirred briskly while she waited for their reaction.

"Oh, well, it's just an old house, and we..."

"We never meant to imply..."

"It's a little creepy, but there's really no such thing..."

Amused, Deegie leaned back in her chair. "Sorry. I won't interrupt anymore. I want the house. Let's just get this done, okay?" And she smiled to show she was sincere. Still, though, it was always a hoot to watch people betray their true feelings against propriety. She sat quietly through the rest of the proceedings, sipping the bitter free coffee and turning down her empath channel. More fake smiles and damp handshakes were exchanged, Deegie's purse was stuffed full of her copies of the agreement, and the house key was now threaded onto her key ring. Once the house was checked for termites and fumigated for venomous spiders, the place would be hers.

She drove back to the house after leaving the realtor's office, hoping to make another attempt to contact the spiritual being inside, but the exterminators had already arrived and were busily covering the old building with bright blue tarps. She sat in the Bus by the side of the road and watched them work for a few minutes, wondering the entire time what effect, if any, the tent fumigation process had on ghosts. The ghastly coffee she'd consumed that morning bubbled and fizzed in her stomach, an unpleasant reminder that she hadn't eaten since sometime last night. A trip to the grocery store was in order.

Minutes later, in the store, she filled a hand basket with apples and oranges. Deegie noticed a familiar face on the other side of the produce department: the redhead with the fake smile from the realty place. She was scowling at the broccoli, and she still wore her Fiddlehead Realty name badge: Stephanie. Deegie watched as Stephanie put down the broccoli, picked up a head of cauliflower, gave it a death glare, then looked up and made eye contact.

"Hi there," Deegie said. "Produce prices are ridiculous, aren't they? It's like we're being punished for wanting to eat healthy, huh?"

"Oh! Hi there!" Stephanie reapplied her fake smile and tossed the cauliflower into her cart. "Yeah, it's, um, pretty expensive, yeah." She fussed with her hair and fiddled with her shopping list, and looked like she wished she were anywhere but here. "Well then. Um, nice seeing you again. Enjoy your new...house..."

Deegie walked around the corner of the citrus fruit display and stood in front of Stephanie's cart, effectively blocking her escape. "Thanks," she replied. "I'm sure I will. Level with me though: why were you and your co-workers so skittery about the house? Did some horrendous event take place there, or something? Come on, tell me. I can take it."

"Well, I don't know, really. I haven't been here long, so maybe you're asking the wrong person. All I know is it's an old house, it's been empty for years, and nobody's shown any interest in it. Now, can I get by, please?" The fake smile wavered, faded, and died on her lips.

"Sorry. And thanks." Deegie stepped aside and let Miss Fakey pass. She must be getting a hefty commission on that house. That would explain her unconvincing lie, anyway. *Or maybe I just give her the creeps,* she thought. When you were the town weirdo, it was bound to happen.

After a quick purchase of sandwich makings, fruit, corn chips, bottled water, and a block of ice for the ice chest, Deegie returned to her peaceful, pine-scented alleyway. Fuming, bruise-colored thunderheads followed her. The storm tore open the sky the minute she parked, and despite the fragrant canopy of the pine boughs over her parking spot, the Bus was drenched in a matter of seconds. Stray pine needles mixed with the downpour and cascaded down the windows. The vehicle's springs creaked as a lively wind gave it a shove, and Deegie discovered a leak in the skylight. Her expression remained serene as she positioned a plastic wastebasket under the drip. A leak was a minor inconvenience when compared to the incredible scent of evergreens bathed in clean mountain rain. She moved to the front of the vehicle and cranked open the vent wing window on the passenger side. Fat raindrops splashed her face as she pulled in a deep breath of the storm's perfume. Her carefully fluffed hair deflated, and her eyeliner ran down her cheeks in ebony trickles. But it wasn't enough. The groceries could be put away later. She needed to immerse herself in this gift from Mother Nature. Deegie got out of the Bus, spread her arms wide, and embraced the deluge.

The unmistakable, high-pitched cry of a kitten in distress cut through the music of the storm, and she stopped her small act of worship, moving handfuls of her dripping black curls away from her ears. The cries came from behind the shop, and she took off in that direction. The cries came from the dumpster that backed up behind The Silent Cat, and Deegie stood on her toes to lift the lid. She took one look and lost her heart to the sad, scrawny creature inside. The kitten was tiny, black, and covered with grease; obviously the victim of someone's cruel prank. The baby looked up at her with brilliant yellow eyes, easily the brightest thing around on this gray day, and let out another plaintive mew.

"Oh crap!" Deegie gasped. "How did you get in there, little guy?"

There was obviously only one way to retrieve the unfortunate kitten from the dumpster, and Deegie hesitated no further. Nimbly, she climbed inside, ripping her black lace skirt and getting foul muck on her boots, but she paid it no mind; a little life needed to be saved. Thunder clapped above them as she clutched the tiny beast to her chest, frightening the little animal, and causing it to deliver a few unintentional scratches to a tender part of Deegie's anatomy. She drew in a sharp breath and did her best to comfort the bedraggled kitten. "Hey," she muttered, "I don't really want pierced nipples! It's okay. Let's get you home."

Once inside the Bus, out of the storm, Deegie examined the kitten for signs of injury. Other than being a little thin and smelling like garbage, the ebony baby seemed to be in good health. She toweled its fur dry with a T-shirt from her laundry bag, rubbing off as much of the slimy, greasy dumpster residue as she could, then summoned a miniature orb of glistening snow-white light. Starting at the kitten's head, she rolled the ball of healing energy over it. The gentle radiance washed over the tiny body, warming it and soothing it until the kitten stopped shivering.

"You must be starved half to death," she said as she looked through her supplies for something that would approximate a meal for a baby feline. "Let's see what I have here...oh! Sliced turkey! Perfect!" Deegie shredded a piece of lunch meat into a lid from a peanut butter jar.

"You're going to need a name, too." Before setting the food down, she picked up the kitten and took a perfunctory glance under its dainty tail. The light in the Bus was dim, the kitten was small, and Deegie only took a quick look. Seeing no evidence of male anatomy, she decided the kitten was female and set it down on the floor, along with the lunch meat in the makeshift dish.

"How about Bastet?" She watched the kitten eat, smiling at its voracious appetite and tiny pointed teeth. "Bast for short. Do you like that name?" The kitten looked up from its meal and meowed loudly, as if in agreement. "I take it that means yes, am I right, Bast?" The kitten swallowed a mouthful of turkey and meowed again.

Deegie was delighted with her new companion, and set about lining the drawer under her narrow bunk with an old towel so Bast would have a bed. While she worked, she continued to talk to the kitten, letting it know how honored it should be to be named after an Egyptian cat Goddess. Throughout the evening, every time she said its name, the kitten mewed loudly and looked up at her with its round golden eyes. Bast politely refused the makeshift bed, preferring to sleep next to Deegie's pillow that night. The black kitten was possessed of a mighty purr, and during the night, Deegie felt the presence and heard the rumble of Tiger Spirit as he checked out the newcomer and patrolled the area.

* * *

"Deegie, you're a walking cliché, you know that?" Zach ran a careful fingertip over Bast's fuzzy head and dangled the string to his sweatshirt hood for the tiny paws to swat at. "Also, you never called me. How come?"

"What do you mean?" Deegie stood at the candle shelves, running a lightly oiled cloth over her wax creations. Muted light gave a mellow gleam to the colorful candles as they stood in their orderly ranks.

"I mean, you never called me. I left my number for you in case you needed help. You got it, right?"

"Yeah, I did get it, and thanks. I was fine. Still am. What I meant was, what do you mean I'm a walking cliché?"

Zach's answer had four parts, and he ticked them off on his fingers as he spoke. "You own a new age shop, I've never seen you in anything but black, you just dumped a shitload of money on a creepy old house, *and* you adopted a black cat. People will start thinking you're a witch or something."

She'd just finished telling him about the house, and Zach had known right away which one she was talking about. He and his brother used to dare each other to look in the windows when they were kids, and they had made up stories about it late at night to frighten themselves.

"A witch, huh?" She stopped what she was doing and appeared to ponder this a moment. "You're probably right about that, but I don't really care what people think." She put down her dust cloth and picked up Bast so she could brush her cheek over the kitten's downy head. "Besides, I wasn't about to leave this baby in that yucky old dumpster." She put Bast down and hovered the steaming tea kettle over Zach's empty cup. "More?"

He shook his head and pointed at the rain-splattered window and the drowned parking lot beyond. "Wish I could, Deeg, but I have to go out in that mess. We'll be going crazy with all the heater repair calls. Happens every time it rains or snows. In the summer, people freak out about their air conditioning. It never ends. It'll probably kill me." He winked to show he was joking, and his pale green eyes twinkled. A moment later, his smile flickered around the edges, and he began toying with a plastic bowl of sugar packets. "Tell you what. Why don't I just buy you dinner tomorrow night, how would that be? You like nachos? We could just do nachos if you want. I know a great Mexican place. No strings, of course," he added, "just as friends." He stopped fiddling with the sugar packets and looked up at her. "What do you say?"

Her left thumb circled her ring finger where the garnet ring had been, and she gave her lower lip a quick nibble. "Sure, Zach," she said. "Nachos sound divine. You can just pick me up here." Her thumb stopped its exploration of her empty finger, and she shoved her hands in the pockets of her skirt. "And thank you." Deegie returned the teakettle to the hotplate and surveyed her customer-free shop. "Looks like I might have a boring day ahead of me. You'd think the magically inclined would enjoy coming out in the rain."

"Wait until it starts snowing. Fiddlehead Creek becomes a ghost town." Zach gulped down the rest of his tea and zipped up his sweatshirt. He hesitated at the door.

Deegie made shooing gestures with both hands. "Go!" she said with a laugh. "The freezing citizens of Fiddlehead Creek demand your presence!"

He flipped up his sweatshirt hood, then, after a deep breath, tipped her a wave and stepped out the door.

Although Zach was the closest thing she had to a friend in Fiddlehead Creek, Deegie felt relieved when his intrepid little Jeep churned through the pine needle-infused puddles in the parking lot and headed off down the main road. While she wasn't exactly non-social, Deegie enjoyed solitude, and sometimes even craved it. Trying to deflect a constant barrage of other peoples' energies and emotions could be exhausting, and she needed a few moments to prepare herself before her customers started to make an appearance. The past few days had been a stress fest, even without the episode of Witch's Cramp.

While the pine-scented rain made music in the puddles, and the old building made its soothing ticks and creaks, she took a few jars of herbs down from their well-dusted shelves and blended a final cup of tea, adding a touch of catnip leaves for a unique, calming touch.

It was surprising how easily she was transitioning from being someone's girlfriend to being a woman on her own. She took this as a sign that this was what she was supposed to do, and she soon found herself wishing she'd done it sooner. This certainly wasn't the first time she'd been thrust out on her own; the first time had been the worst.

The circumstances had been indelibly etched into her mind, so close to the surface that they came back to her and tormented her sleep every now and then. She remembered listening to an Evanescence CD and rolling her eyes at a pile of homework when the sounds of her parents' cocktail party took on an ominous tone: her mother's voice, screaming out part of a spell before being abruptly choked off; her father's bellow of outrage and pain; and the deep, guttural battle cries of Tiger Spirit as he struggled with an unseen assailant in the living room. The dinner guests ran screaming into the street. Deegie dove for the closet and folded her small body into the darkness behind a set of luggage and a cedar chest. She stayed there for what must have been hours, alternating between silent desperate sobbing and sweaty, fitful sleep. Tiger paced back and forth in front of the closet door, restless and edgy and endlessly growling. The rest of the house had gone utterly silent.

When she awoke to find Moley staring placidly at her from the open closet door, she hadn't the strength left to scream. She gazed back at him with red, swollen eyes and simply said, "I suppose you'll kill me too now."

But he hadn't. He'd introduced himself as Mr. Hack and called himself an agent of her father's, a title he never elaborated on. After allowing her to pack only a few things, he took her away from the house and gave her only a brief description of what had happened during her parents' fateful cocktail party.

"An assassin was sent. Your father was the target; your mother simply got in the way, and if you'd been found, you would have been killed too. Roland Tibbs should have known better than to attempt to leave the Dark Flock. It's a lifetime obligation, unfortunately, and there can be collateral damage. You will be given money from your parents' estate on the last day of every month. I will find you, no matter where you are. Tell no one, ever. There is always a chance you will be the next target." Moley regarded her without pity. "Especially if your father has taught you things you shouldn't know."

Wisely, she'd kept her mouth shut. She knew more about her father's secrets than she would ever admit.

That was all Moley would ever say regarding the deaths of her parents. Deegie was loaded into his car and rode in silence for the better part of three days before arriving in San Francisco, almost 1,200 miles away from the only home she'd ever known. Moley arranged an apartment for her, a cramped, brooding studio in the Tenderloin District. From there, she led a fairly solitary life, had few friends and even fewer boyfriends. She supplemented the posthumous monthly allowance from her parents and kept herself busy with the occasional job, took classes at the community college, met and almost married Spencer, and opened her own business.

Memories of her parents and childhood faded, became yellowed around the edges, but never disappeared, and Deegie took them out and replayed them on the movie screen of her mind on long nights when sleep eluded her. As the years went by, there was one question that still remained unanswered, something else that demanded her attention on those sleepless nights: exactly who or what had killed her parents? Moley had never told her, despite repeated questioning.

The shop's phone ruined the peaceful tranquility of the stormy morning, and upon answering, Deegie learned that the rain would delay the tent fumigation of her house for another three days at least. Back to the gypsy lifestyle whether she liked it or not. She'd taped Zach's business card to the wall next to the phone, and she ran a fingertip over the number. *Maybe,* she thought. *Maybe if things get really uncomfortable. And no strings attached. Not a single one.*

* * *

The next morning, Deegie took Bast into the local veterinarian's office for a complete check-up. After examining her and giving the kitten a clean bill of health, the vet gave Deegie a few pointers on kitten care and suggested a date to bring her pet back for neutering. "It's best to get males fixed as soon as they are old enough," the vet said. "That way, they're less inclined to wander away from home, and they aren't as likely to pee all over everything."

"Male?" Deegie frowned. "You mean Bast is a boy?" In response to hearing its name again, the kitten mewed enthusiastically.

"Oh yes," the vet replied with a knowing smile, "a little male, about five weeks old. It's hard to tell when they're this young."

"Oh boy. I was *sure* this was a girl kitty! I'd already given it a girl's name. I guess I'll have to call you something else then. Right Bast?"

Meew! said Bast.

Deegie picked up Bast from the examination table and nuzzled his fur. Either way, the little guy was going to be a wonderful comfort to her. She thanked the vet, paid the bill, then bought a bag of kitten food, litter, and a plastic litter box from the pet shop next door. She made it to the shop two minutes before opening time.

At noon, she closed The Silent Cat for a lunch break and drove out to her future new home. The image of the ghost and its plaintive whisper as it struggled to manifest in the hall had not left her mind, and she felt compelled to attempt contact again, even if she couldn't enter the house to do so. She sat parked across the street with Bast in her lap, feeding him kitten kibble piece by piece, and letting her mind drift past the striped fumigation tarps to the darkened, cobweb-strewn interior of the house. Her head lolled to one side, and her eyes drifted shut. She was aware of the purring kitten on her lap, the sharp yet dainty claws in her leg, and the tireless patter of the rain on the roof of the Bus, but in her mind, she roamed the gloomy hallway, oblivious to the haze of insecticide, searching for the lost soul who wandered there too. It was rather enjoyable, just letting her mind wander and search. Unlike the release of magical energy, this didn't hurt at all.

A woman's voice, lilting in song, drifted down the hallway. The sound was muffled and tinny, like listening to the voices of long-dead singers on an antique Victrola, and Deegie strained to hear the words; they faded in and out like forgotten ideas.

"Hello? Who are you?" Deegie sent the thought spinning into the dusty house, and the eerie singing stopped.

We sing together. All of us on guard...

"What? I don't understand. Tell me more."

The glass must not break...never break it...

"I'm sorry, I still don't understand."

The ghost made a sad whimpering sound, as if she were frustrated by her inability to clarify her meaning. *I am in the garden,* she sighed. *The kitties bring me comfort*

Deegie heard the familiar warning rumble of Tiger Spirit now, and she smelled his wild scent. Her concentration wavered and she lost contact. She jerked out of her trance and sat up straighter as the interior of the Bus came into focus. Bast still perched on her lap, licking his whiskers with an expectant look on his furry face, and in the living quarters behind her, she heard the *ploink ploink ploink* of the skylight leak dripping into the wastebasket.

"Tiger, what is it? I feel no threat from her at all. What's gotten you so riled up lately?"

The Bus shuddered and rocked as Tiger Spirit tried to pace in its close quarters, and the rear windows fogged over behind their tie-dyed curtains. Deegie had never known him to be so restless; not even when she had first hooked up with Spencer had Tiger been so uneasy. Something about the house seemed to be troubling him a great deal, but she had no earthly idea of what it could be. All that house needed was some paint, some furniture, and some love. She sensed nothing negative about it at all.

Maybe it's just the newness of it all, she thought. *Tiger's always been kind of a mother hen.*

She started the Bus' engine and navigated through the steady rain back to her secluded alley. Only when the house was a distant speck in the rear-view mirror did Tiger return to the Spirit World. It was at times like this when Deegie wished Tiger could actually speak with her. It was his job to protect her from harm and to provide comfort, and he had been there for her when she had absolutely no one to turn to, but it would be nice if he were able to explain his sometimes erratic behavior instead of her having to guess the reasons for it.

CHAPTER FOUR

DOS HOMBRES CANTINA WAS DARK and atmospheric. Candles in glass jars illuminated the tiny round tables in the dining area, and the enticing aromas of salsa and frying meat hung heavy in the air. A long mahogany bar took up one side of the building, and perky, college-age waitresses in red and yellow aprons scurried about, carrying serving trays filled with pitchers of margaritas and draft beer.

Deegie sailed past the bar, deliberately ignoring the lecherous grin of a crusty-looking old gent perched on a stool at the very end. "Let's sit back there," she said to Zach, pointing to the sparsely populated dining room. "Fewer creepies back there, if you catch my drift. Well, besides me, of course." She shook her head, making her silver skull earrings jingle, then laughed nervously at her own silliness.

She settled herself at the tiny table, adjusting her skirt, stowing her purse, and hoping Zach wouldn't go beyond small talk. The last thing she wanted to do was fend off the advances of a wannabe suitor while she was still recovering from the mess with Spencer.

One of the perky waitresses jiggled up to their table, order pad in hand, and she greeted Zach with an overly enthusiastic "Zach! Omigawd! Hiiii!" To Deegie she only offered a perfunctory "Hi," and a considerably toned-down smile.

After the waitress took their order and bounced away, Deegie raised an eyebrow and gave Zach a knowing smirk. "So you're a regular here, I see."

Zach's blush was almost as red as his beard. "Oh yeah, I come here on payday sometimes. I don't know her, though. I mean I know her, but I don't *know* her. Just from here, you know?"

Amused by Zach's charming awkwardness, Deegie stopped her gentle teasing and took another look around at the restaurant's décor: colorful, primitive paintings on the faux adobe walls; authentic, beaded sombreros over their table; artificial cacti in red clay pots.

And the scroungy-looking guy at the end of the bar, still staring intently at her.

She glared back at him, her face deliberately grim, then returned her attention to Zach. "Interesting gentleman," she said. "Is he a regular too?"

"Oh, him." Zach looked at the man without being obvious about it. "Yeah, he's here a lot. He's one of our local characters. People call him Shit Storm Murphy. I don't know what his real name is, though. Got a little taste for the sauce, if you know what I mean."

"So I see."

"He's a little off, but he's harmless. Likes to get drunk and tell tall tales, but nobody really believes them."

"He likes to stare, that's for sure."

"Can't say I blame him." Zach said.

Miss Perky reappeared with their food, saving Deegie the trouble of coming up with a reply. The order of nachos came on a plate the size of a Thanksgiving turkey platter and took up most of the table. Once the delectable aroma hit her nose, Deegie realized she was famished and dug in immediately, further delaying any more conversation. She felt the licentious gaze of Shit Storm Murphy creep over her body on one side, and Zach's nervous, bashful energy on the other. She kept her eyes on the olives, melted cheese, and sour cream, and wished she'd ordered a margarita instead of an iced tea.

From the corner of her eye, she saw Murphy heave his considerable bulk off his bar stool and begin weaving his way on unsteady legs towards their table. "Great," she muttered around a mouthful of tortilla chips. "Here he comes."

Zach's expression was pained as the colorful drunk shambled up to them. "Hey Murph. Can we talk later, bud? Kinda having dinner with my friend here."

"Yer friend, eh?" Murphy's voice was rough and burbling from long years of alcohol and tobacco abuse, and he was redolent with the odors of stale beer and unwashed armpits. "I know her too!"

"No you don't!" Deegie snapped, and she covered her nose with her hand and looked pleadingly at Zach.

Murphy's riotous laughter stopped conversation at the bar; patrons turned on their stools to see what the matter was. "Sure I do! You're the gal who bought the old place at the end of Fox Lane! I was takin' a little snooze in the trees, and I seen ya movin' in!" He slapped his thighs and cackled laughter. "Hey, dintcha used to live over on High Street once? Huh? You did, dintcha! See you got ya a new beau!"

"Oh shit," said Deegie.

"Murph, come on now..." said Zach.

Murphy lowered his voice to a more conversational level. "Aw, don't worry, Miss. I won't hurt ya." He paused, as if trying to convince himself of this. "I'll let ya be. Say, you *do* know what went on up there way back when, don't ya? Up at yer new place?"

Zach leaned into Shit Storm Murphy's stink cloud and lowered his voice. "Look, Murph. You need to be nice tonight. I mean it. This is a very nice lady here, and she's a good friend of mine."

"No, wait." Deegie shook her head and patted Zach's arm. Having a ghost in the house was something she was looking forward to. Murphy's tale of way back when might just give her a little more information on how that ghost came to be there in the first place. Besides, in spite of the discomfort he was causing her nose, she sensed no ill will from him.

"It's okay, Zach," she said. "Who knows, a little history on my old place might be interesting."

She looked up at Murphy. "Go ahead and tell me—quickly—then you have to go back to the bar and let us eat, deal?" (Deegie's appetite had dulled considerably, but she certainly didn't want this guy hanging out at their table).

"Yes ma'am." Murphy grinned and picked at the seat of his overalls, and he slid his bleary eyes from Deegie to Zach and back again before beginning his tale. "Seems there was some odd doings in that house back in the nineteen twenty-odds. Two brothers. Folks back then say them boys actually conjured up a livin' demon. At least that's what my daddy used to tell me. Some folks say you can still hear that accursed thing screamin' in the woods in the middle of the night." He peered at Deegie from beneath bushy grey brows. "You just take care in there, missy. My daddy tole me some gawd-awful stuff went on up in that house."

"Really? Like what?" Deegie put down her half-eaten chip and leaned forward.

"Well, them two brothers was found dead right there in the livin' room by the fireplace. Seems they just couldn't live with what they done, callin' up the devil and all. Boom! They blew their own fool heads off!" He scratched his grizzled beard and looked perplexed then. "Or maybe it was hangin'. Yeah, that's it. They done hung themselves. Sometimes I forget. Like to drink, ya know."

"Great." Deegie dropped her chip back onto the plate and rolled her eyes. "Thanks for the heads up." Zach was right. This guy was full of sauce and full of crap. There was a presence in the house, sure, but the ghost and her cats were far from evil.

"I haven't heard *anything* about that house, and I've lived here all my life," Zach said. "It's just an old house that's been sitting there longer than any of us have been around, Murph. Are you sure you weren't just dreaming that up to scare Deegie?"

"Nope! Wouldn't do that! I remember everything my uncle told me, and that's a fact!"

"Uncle? Wait, I thought it was your *dad* who told you." Deegie drew herself back into her chair as far as she could. "Never mind. Thanks for the entertainment, Mr. Shit Storm. You can go back to your beer now."

Murphy offered a sheepish grin. "I just thought you ought to know," he said, and reached out for her shoulder with a grubby paw.

In one swift, instinctive motion, Deegie brought her hand up and snapped her fingers. A spark of pale blue lit up the dark table like a mini-flashbulb, and Murphy jumped back with a yelp.

"Damn static 'lectricity!" he sputtered. "Dang, girl, you wearin' wool or something? You 'bout blew me outta my shoes!"

"Sorry." Deegie didn't mean it, of course; she wasn't sorry at all. Brief pain flickered in her head, reminding her of her disability, but small energy expenditures weren't too bad. She was good for another small zap or two before the real pain set in. Her hand stayed poised in front of her on the table, middle finger to thumb, ready to deliver another painful zap should he be bold enough to touch her again. *Go ahead, you nasty old thing,* she thought, *touch me again and see what happens.*

Murphy shuffled back to the bar, only to be patiently escorted out by the bartender. He went willingly enough, waving to the other patrons, and declaring his undying love for all who witnessed his inebriated antics. The Shit Storm Murphy Show was over for the day.

Deegie ran quick fingers through her thick black curls and scowled as Murphy was led away.

"Wow that was some shock! *Are* you wearing wool or something?" Zach gaped at her from across the pile of nachos.

"Oh, no, no, I—it's my hair. It gets all full of static in the fall. It's the curls or something, I don't know." She shrugged as if she were puzzled herself, and changed the subject. "Hey, our munchies are getting cold! Let's dig in!" She scooped up chips and melted cheese with an enthusiasm she hoped was convincing; the last thing she wanted to do right now was eat.

"Aw, hey, Deeg, I'm real sorry about this," Zach lowered his voice and poked at an olive slice. "I completely forgot about Murph. I hope he didn't ruin everything. I mean, that story didn't freak you out or anything, did it?"

Relief flooded her chest, and she let her shoulders drop. He was more concerned with their disrupted non-date than he was with the accidental display of magic that had just taken place right in front of him. "No. I'm fine. People embellish stories to fit their own need, or they just make them up altogether. Happens all the time. I'm fine, Zach."

"Well...okay then. Hey, it's still early; we could go get a coffee or something after we finish here. Hammond's is just right around the corner. Great coffee, tempting desserts, just like the commercial says."

Deegie feigned skepticism. "No pumpkin spice or candy cane sprinkles, I hope? No chatty drunken bums?"

"Nope. Just plain old coffee. Or tea if you want; they have that too. So, is that a yes?"

"Throw in a slice of pie, and you've got a deal."

Over peach pie and strong coffee, Zach gleaned a few more details about the enigmatic Deegie Tibbs from The Silent Cat: she was an only child, she practiced aromatherapy, she liked to go camping by herself, she once had a boa constrictor named Silent Sam, and she wanted to open a refuge for homeless cats.

"I think the backyard of my new place would be a perfect cat hang-out if I had it fenced in. And there are plenty of rooms I could use for indoor kitties, too. It's going to rock, you'll see." She cut into a peach slice with the side of her fork and briefly debated whether or not to tell him about the ghost.

"You really are serious about living there, aren't you?" Zach pushed aside his empty plate and leaned forward on his elbows.

"Spooky old houses and rumors of demonology don't freak you out?"

"Don't forget creepy drunk guys hiding in the woods watching me move in!" Deegie added with a wink. "But no, it doesn't freak me out, not really. It's just an old house, and old houses almost always have some sort of urban legend attached to them. I'm guessing nobody's lived there for quite some time."

"That place had been empty since I was a kid. Someone would come and check on it from time to time, but no one ever moved in."

"Well, the neighborhood will get used to me sooner or later," Deegie said. "Because that house is perfect for me, and I'm not going anywhere."

Later, when he brought her back to the Bus and her cozy, tree-lined alley behind The Silent Cat, Zach tried once more to offer Deegie the use of his guest room. She declined, gently, and pointed to the windows of the Bus, where Bast peered out from behind the purple tie-dyed curtains. "I have to feed that little guy," she said. "And I'll be fine, so don't worry."

"Alright, then. See you in the morning, as usual?"

"Yup." She considered kissing his cheek, dismissed the thought, then let herself out of the Jeep. "And thanks again for the nachos."

* * *

Deegie paid to have the house painted; that task was far too daunting for one person. While the four-man crew busied themselves with tarps, ladders, scaffolds, and five-gallon buckets of white paint, Deegie retreated to the neglected and overgrown backyard. She could already imagine a nice vegetable and herb garden here, and there was room for a gazebo as well. In her mind's eye, she could see herself completely at ease in her newly landscaped backyard, perhaps lying in a gently swaying hammock while spring breezes brushed cool unseen fingers through her unruly black hair. She ripped the tags from a new pair of leather gloves and put them on, not quite sure where to begin. Zach had lent her some gardening implements from his own tool shed: a heavy set of pruners, a hack saw, a shovel and hoe. She'd challenged herself to get at least half of the backyard clear of weeds and brambles by lunch time, and she decided to start at the far corner and make her way back to the house.

After an hour or so, Deegie wondered what she'd gotten herself into. She was sweating profusely despite the coolness of the day, her cheeks were beginning to tingle with the first signs of sunburn, and her forearms were laddered and crisscrossed with angry red scratches from thorns and sharp twigs. She sat back on her heels, gulping thirstily from a thermos of iced tea she'd brought with her, and wondered what on earth Bast was up to.

Earlier, the black kitten had been lounging in the shade of the pink marble bird-bath, watching Deegie intently with his sleepy golden eyes. Now he crept across the dry, yellowed grass with infinite slowness, the way cats do when they are stalking something. He stopped about a foot from an overgrown box hedge and hunkered down on his belly. Only the tip of his tail moved now; it flicked up and down, rattling dried leaves together with a stealthy crinkle. *A bird, or perhaps a small animal, is hiding out in that bush*, Deegie thought.

Just as she was about to scold Bast for threatening an innocent creature, something that looked very much like a tattered puff of gray smoke drifted out of the hedge at ground level, then wafted its way over to Bast. Deegie frowned and shaded her eyes with her hand, then took off her sunglasses and scrubbed them with the edge of her AC/DC T-shirt. She put them back on and still saw the anomaly, more clearly now in fact. It was a small cloud of diaphanous...stuff...about the size of a football, and as she watched, part of it stretched out from itself and waved back and forth, looking for all the world like a cat's fluffy tail. Four legs began to take shape, cat's legs, she was sure of it, then a triangular feline head, complete with a sweet little face and upright, pointy ears. Its paws were soundless as the spirit cat closed the distance between itself and Bast, who lifted a forepaw, as if in greeting, then began to purr. The two of them touched their noses together, as cats will do when they are friendly with one another, then the ghostly cat turned away from Bast and dashed full speed across the yard. Then, before the wondering eyes of the cat and his human, it faded into nothingness.

Deegie sat spellbound for a long moment, her heartbeat thundering in her ears, and her rapt smile still frozen in place. Bast returned to his spot by the bird bath, licked his paws as if nothing out of the ordinary had taken place, then curled into himself to resume his nap. Deegie got up and hurried across the lawn, then knelt next to the hedge into which the ghost cat had appeared. Next to it was a wild tangle of weeds, brambles, leaves, and garden debris, and when she looked closer, she saw small, irregularly shaped objects sticking out of the soft black earth. Unmindful of the sharp thorns, she began clearing away the debris, and a few moments later she sat back on the long-dead grass, looking at her discovery. She didn't even feel the scratches on her arms.

She had uncovered miniature headstones, more than a dozen of them, some made of wood, some of stone, and all carefully lettered with the names of pets: Muffin, Fancy, Rusty, Squeak, and others, some barely legible. Deegie had discovered a long-forgotten pet cemetery in her backyard. There were dates on some of the stones, one dating back to 1905, three years after the house had been built. The witch was touched beyond belief by the loving manner in which the previous occupants had laid their beloved animal companions to rest, and she vowed to preserve and care for this little cemetery in the best way she knew how. This was a good omen for sure; this was the perfect place for a cat sanctuary, and as far as she was concerned, it was just one more reason to love this old house.

* * *

With the last of her savings, Deegie purchased used furniture from a thrift shop, including a wonderful velvet patchwork couch of all colors. In the living room, now tucked behind the couch, were two oil paintings, one of a colonial-looking man in navy blue, and one of a red-haired woman in pink. While they weren't professional, she'd taken an instant liking to them and bought them as well, thinking they would look right at home in the entryway. She bought a new stove and refrigerator on sale at Taylor's Appliance on Morris Street and filled the refrigerator with enough food for a week.

The electricity had been turned on, but the heating oil tank, which was supposed to have been filled today, was still bone-dry, which meant no heat tonight, except for a small, elderly space heater. The pipes hadn't been used in decades, and the faucets produced only a slow trickle of odd-smelling, root-beer-colored water. One more thing that would have to wait until tomorrow. Thank goodness she'd had the presence of mind to purchase two cases of bottled water that day.

Deegie sat cross-legged on her mattress on the floor—she had been far too exhausted to assemble the bed frame—and she sipped a cup of lukewarm cocoa while going over what remained of her to-do list. She had not seen or sensed the ghost since moving in, but that didn't surprise her; ghosts had a way of laying low while the living moved in and got settled. The spectral being that sang to her hadn't gone far. Bast lay curled beside her, nose to tail, purring as usual. Bast always purred, whether he had reason to or not. Her hand reached out for his little black body, and she buried her fingers in his fur. At least he would be warm tonight. She pulled a sweatshirt on over her pink penguin pajamas and kept a wary eye on the old-fashioned electrical outlet as she turned up the space heater a notch. The building inspector had declared the wiring perfectly safe, but she always half-expected a shower of blue sparks and immediate electrocution every time she plugged something in. The heater's hum went up an octave, and the coils glowed a brighter orange.

Deegie rubbed her hands together in front of the increased heat, then returned her attention to her list. There were only a few items left on it, and she was quite pleased with herself for managing to have such a productive day. One of the items that still needed to be checked off was number four: Find the key to the basement. The realtor had told her that the key, a charmingly old-fashioned one, could be found hanging on an equally charming old-fashioned nail located next to the kitchen door. Alas, the nail was there, but the key was not, and that bothered Deegie a great deal. The basement was the only area of the house that she hadn't explored. The attic had been no big deal, mostly cobwebs and dust, but there was something about not seeing the basement that nagged at her.

She gulped down the last of her cocoa and decided to search the kitchen one more time before attempting to sleep. That damn key had to be around here somewhere. She got up from her mattress, leaving her curled-up kitty sound asleep on her pillow, and shuffled into the kitchen, her bunny slippers slippy-slapping across the hardwood floor. The key was nowhere to be found, not on any nail, not in any drawer, not anywhere. What she did find was a screwdriver, along with a butter knife and an old knitting needle. One way or another, she was getting into that blasted basement tonight.

She was surprised by how easily she was able to pick the old lock; it had only taken a minute or two. She pushed on the thick wooden door, and the hinges shrieked and groaned theatrically as it opened. A veil of ancient cobwebs stretched across the entryway, and after knocking them down with a broom, Deegie stepped over the threshold. She only saw the first four steps of the basement staircase; the rest disappeared into inky blackness. An antique push-button light switch was on the wall to her right, and she laughed in surprise when it actually worked. The room below her was illuminated by a sickly yellow light, and, still holding onto her web-whacking broom, Deegie descended the creaky wooden staircase.

The light down here wasn't much, just a couple of forty-watt bulbs hanging by raw, dangerous-looking wires. The corners of the basement were still in deep pockets of shadow, and it didn't take much imagination to conjure up images of raggedy, bulging-eyed basement creatures, things that hadn't seen light in years. A stack of moldering cardboard boxes leaned precariously next to a jumble of ancient, broken furniture that smelled of cat pee and stale cigarette smoke. A long wooden table sat at the far end of the basement, and Deegie saw that it held row upon row of what appeared to be canning jars, each with a paper label. The table and its jars were covered with a layer of dust and grime so thick that Deegie's hands immediately turned a sooty black the minute she picked up the first jar and began to look it over. The label was yellowed and peeling, but there was just enough light for her to read what it said: Golden Chain. The jar was empty, but she could see some sort of milky white residue at the bottom. Strange. Golden Chain was once used in ancient medicines and magical spells. It was highly poisonous.

The next jar was labeled Roots of Both Hellebores, another poisonous magical ingredient no one used anymore. Deegie frowned, wondering just what she'd discovered here in the freezing cold basement of her old house. Any magical practitioner worth their salt knew better than to mess with this stuff. Anyone practicing white magic, that is.

I think that old drunk was telling the truth! She remembered the pages of her father's Book of Shadows, which she'd accidently found one day as a child and read in secret every chance she got. Poisonous herbs and roots were always used in spells for summoning demons.

She put down Roots of Both Hellebores and reached for another jar at random. This one was even filthier than the others, and it bore no label. When she gave it a gentle shake, something rattled and clinked against the glass. The lid was rusted tight; she was unable to wrench it open, but when she stood directly under one of the hanging light bulbs and wiped away some of the grime, she was able to see what was inside.

Five severed human fingers, withered, gray, and nearly fleshless, lay in a cluster at the bottom of the jar.

Deegie nearly dropped the jar and its gruesome contents in her haste to return it to its spot on the table. What kind of weirdo kept dried severed fingers in a jar? Not surprisingly, the basement was now the last place on earth she wanted to be. She backed away from the table, casting her eyes around the dim basement. The shadows loomed in long-forgotten corners, as if they were indignant about having their space invaded by this ordinary human who eschewed severed fingers and the Roots of Both Hellebores.

At the top of the stairs, Tiger Spirit roared, sounding agitated again, and Deegie took the stairs two at a time, her pumping legs a blur of motion. Once at the top, she slapped at the light switch until the basement went dark again, then slammed the door as hard as she could.

CHAPTER FIVE

ONCE BACK IN HER FREEZING bedroom, Deegie sat cross-legged on her mattress with the blankets draped cloak-like over her shoulders and Bast curled in a fuzzy, purring bundle on her lap. She held Zach's business card and her cell phone in hands that trembled slightly, and she argued with herself over whether or not to call him right then and there. She had no reason to be afraid of a bunch of old jars full of poisonous herbs and severed fingers; she'd seen and dealt with much worse in her twenty-seven years. But there had been great evil in that basement at one time, and the remnants of that baleful energy still lingered in the damp, forgotten room. She tucked her phone and Zach's card back into the side pocket of her purse; she would accept his offer of assistance tomorrow, when he came into the shop for his newspaper and tea.

In Deegie's mind, the next logical step would be another attempt to contact the spirit that roamed the house. If a close enough attraction were formed, she might be able to glean some information from the singing ghost as to what had taken place in the basement. The instant the thought came to her, Tiger Spirit bellowed again. He wasn't in the room with her, but paced the hall outside the partially closed door; she heard the rasp of huge paws on the wooden floor and the singular grunt and rumble of the big cat. Bast raised his head and watched the doorway, attentive, but unafraid. Deegie still found it odd that Tiger had come to her so often lately. Although he had been her guardian since birth, there were occasions when he didn't appear for weeks at a time.

Perhaps he sensed the residual energy in the basement too. She veiled herself and Bast in white light and sent out a silent greeting to the timid ghost.

She heard the singing again, muffled and eerie, and once more Deegie strained to make out the words. It sounded like an aria in an opera and was vaguely familiar. The indistinct melody wafted down the hall, and she felt the presence of the ghost cat she'd seen in the garden, then several more, followed by the singing ghost herself. Deegie sensed a roiling ball of energy at the end of the hall: the ghost woman and the purring, mewing shades of a dozen or so long-deceased cats. Tiger Spirit grunted and huffed, his invisible body still stationed at the bedroom doorway as he protected his mistress.

We cannot pass...

The voice was a puff of cold air in Deegie's ear, and it carried an edge of despair and regret: Tiger Spirit was blocking any further contact. The spirit could communicate, but Tiger would not let her come near.

He is my guardian, Deegie sent out her reply. Despite the chill of the room, beads of sweat glistened on her forehead. *He is only trying to keep me safe. I am Deegie. Who are you and what is in the basement?*

We sing together. All of us on guard...

I don't understand. What is your name?

The purring and mewing of the ghost cats increased. Deegie smelled warm fur, and litter box, and the dried meat smell of kibble.

Elisabeth. I am Lisbet...Lisbet...we cannot pass...

Tiger Spirit's deafening roar thundered throughout the house. Contact, tenuous to begin with, was snapped, lost, and the ghost (*Lisbet...Lisbet...*) faded, along with her feline companions. Deegie's concentration dissolved, and her brilliant net of white light snuffed out. Bast hissed and dove under the bed sheet with his tail fluffed to three times its normal size.

"Tiger! Why did you do that? I only wanted to talk to her! She's harmless!" She was dismayed, but Deegie knew the mighty guardian spirit had his reasons. Through the partially open doorway, she saw the rose-print wallpaper ripple as though it were briefly underwater, and Tiger Spirit huffed, uttered a rough purr, and vanished too.

Deegie awoke later, just as the full moon reached its apex in the night sky. She experienced the brief "where the hell am I?" sensation one gets when waking up in a new place, and when it passed, she sat up in bed, groggy and wondering what had awakened her. The kitten was a fuzzy sleeping ball next to her pillow; Bast hadn't disturbed her sleep. The floor was freezing under her bare feet as she went to the window and looked out at the yard. Shrubbery, a pile of leaves, and a few gardening tools lay bathed in bluish-white moonbeams, but nothing moved. Ordinarily, she would have disregarded the annoying experience and gone back to bed, but something beckoned to her then, called to her without words, and after a moment's concentration, she pinpointed its source: the basement.

"Lisbet? Is that you?"

There was no reply from the frail little spirit she'd communicated with earlier, but the restive energy from the bowels of the house continued to pull at her, needing her, requesting her presence. Deegie tugged on a robe and slippers, and, shivering, heeded its unarticulated call once more.

The basement lights blew out with a loud pop when she pressed the button on the old-fashioned light switch, but she was undaunted and determined once again to venture down into the dark depths beneath the house. The kitchen was to the right of the basement door, and, taking advantage of the moonlight that poured through the window, Deegie located her flashlight in the utility drawer. She flicked it on and shone its powerful beam down the old wooden stairs.

Those shadows again, like angular, curious heads turning in her direction and wondering what she wanted this time. Deegie paid them little mind; they were unsettling, but she knew they were only shadows. Veiled in her own protective light, she held the flashlight in front of her like a weapon and shone it on the nicked and filthy wooden table against the far wall. The cluster of grimy canning jars, with their garlands of spider webs and coating of thick dust, sat waiting for her on the tabletop. This is where it came from, that insistent pull; that irresistible, voiceless call. Deegie obeyed, suddenly finding herself unable to do otherwise. She crouched before the table, eye level with the collection of jars, and she reached out for the one in the very center: the one holding the withered remains of five human fingers.

Something moved inside the jar. Specks of black dust whirled and twined around the dried fingers, making a stealthy, slithering sound, and turning the jar and its contents into a macabre snow globe saturated with dark energies. A red, slit-pupiled eye appeared in the center and peered out at Deegie, and, entranced and unable to help herself, she put her fingers on the rusty lid, ready to open it.

A rush of warm air and an unearthly growl dissolved the strange trance that Deegie had slipped into. The jar slipped from her grasp and fell on its side, mere inches away from the edge of the table. Tiger burst through the membrane between the worlds in a furious whirlwind, and Deegie felt his fangs graze her skin as he seized her by the pajama bottoms and dragged her towards the staircase. With his huge head, he urged her up the risers, none too gently, and when she reached the top, a final shove sent her sprawling across the floor. He circled her, uttering his distinct grunt and rumble, and nudged her until she got to her feet.

"Tiger! What the hell are you doing?" She braced herself against the wall, brushing handfuls of hair away from her face and staring in bewilderment at the open basement door. She had a vague recollection of going down there, but the reason escaped her.

Was I sleepwalking?

She closed the basement door and found herself wishing it had several more locks. Tiger Spirit seethed against her legs; she felt his steamy breath against her bare feet. "All right, all right, I'm going."

Baffled and drowsy, she headed back to her room, and bed, and Bast, wondering what in the hell had just happened.

Exhaustion and stress. That has to be it. I was just dreaming, simply sleepwalking. Go back to sleep, Deeg.

Back in her room, sleep eluded her. Deegie lay in bed, awake and alert, and watched the pine branches shift in the breeze just outside her window. Sometime before dawn, she caught the faint, ethereal voice of Lisbet singing to her cats.

* * *

The Silent Cat would not open for another hour, but Deegie already had the register stocked and the shelves dusted. A full pot of hot water sat waiting to be poured over tea bags, and Zach would be here soon. She'd texted instead of calling, telling him to meet her at the shop before it opened. She wasn't ready to reveal her true nature to him, but she certainly needed someone to listen to her fantastic tale, and, hopefully, to help her clear away the gruesome artifacts in the basement. She didn't want to touch those jars again, didn't even want to look at them. While she waited, she briefly considered moving back into the Bus until all the junk was out of the basement and it had been cleansed, both physically and psychically, but it was only a passing thought; that house was rightfully hers now and she had every right to be there. Besides, Tiger Spirit was always on guard. Deegie heard the distinctive sound of the Jeep's engine and saw the Greenpeace flag flickering through the screen of trees, then spotted the bright red of Zach's beard as he drove through the puddles in the parking lot. She unlocked the door, opened it, and waited for him.

"Hey." Zach's greeting was hesitant and his face bore a look of extreme concern as he entered The Silent Cat. "What happened? Everything okay?"

"Of course," Deegie said as she locked the door. "If I weren't okay, I'd have called instead of texted." She brought over the kettle and filled their cups, then sat down opposite him. "I just need to tell you a couple of things, both creepy as hell. Okay?"

He nodded, bobbing his tea bag up and down in the cup. "Yeah. Go ahead. I like creepy things."

After a long breath, she said, "Looks like ol' Shit Splat, or whatever his name is, was telling us the truth. Sort of. I found jars and jars of poisonous herbs in the basement, the kind used in raising demons. Looks like they've been down there for decades."

"Well, that *is* kind of strange, but they're just jars of herbs, right? Maybe someone had an herb garden, or something like that. Doesn't mean they were raising demons."

"There's more." She curled her own fingers into her hands, as though she were protecting them. "There's another jar with human fingers in it. Mummified ones, all shriveled up."

"Fingers?" Zach cringed and stopped bobbing his tea bag. "Seriously? Actual fingers?"

"Yeah. You know nothing good was going on down there in that basement." Her hands went to her forearms, trying to smooth down the goose bumps that rose there. "There's also the ghost of an old lady, and about a dozen ghost cats, give or take. I'm not making it up, I swear."

Zach smirked. "You're not trying to pull a Shit Storm Murphy on me?"

"I'm not. Swear. The house is definitely haunted, and there are severed fingers in the basement."

Zach said nothing for a moment, and Deegie was beginning to think he considered her a nut case after all, when he finally spoke. "I think you should talk to my brother."

Deegie narrowed her eyes. "Why?"

"He knows all about this stuff. He's kind of like a—well, you'll see. To me, that sounds dangerous as hell. Stay out of that basement until I can get over there and get rid of that stuff for you. I'll bring Gilbert along so you can meet him. He'll know what to do, don't worry." He stood up to go, then added, "You two have the exact same color eyes. It's uncanny."

Deegie felt better for having told Zach about her predicament, at least in part. "Thank you, Zach. You're a true friend, and no, I won't go anywhere near the basement." That last part was the complete truth. Deegie had no desire to ever go down there again.

It was agreed that the Altman brothers would come to Deegie's house that evening, and the first order of business would be the removal of the jars from the basement. Deegie supposed she could have done this herself, and she chided herself a little for being so freaked out, but it would feel better having someone there to help her. Two someones, now. She was looking forward to meeting Gilbert, and seeing just how much he "knew about this stuff."

CHAPTER SIX

ZACH AND GILBERT ALTMAN ARRIVED at Deegie's house just as the sun was going down, and when Deegie opened the door to greet them, they were silhouetted by a glorious sunset of purple and gold, the colors of royalty. She took this as a good omen, and let them in. Gilbert was a little shorter and two years younger than his brother, but his hair was every bit as red. When she met his eyes, Deegie saw that Zach was correct: they were the exact shade of pale ice-blue as her own. Despite the still-hectic and unpacked condition of her home, she greeted them confidently enough, and ushered them into the living room.

Before he seated himself on Deegie's couch, he surveyed the room, head cocked to the side as if he were listening to something. "There are quite a few entities in here," he said as he slowly lowered himself to the couch.

Deegie frowned. "One. Unless you count the—"

"Cats? Is that what I feel?" Gilbert leaned forward and peered down the long hallway. His smile wavered around the edges. "And is that the basement door down there?"

"Yes, and yes." Deegie glanced over at Zach, who shook his head and shrugged.

"I didn't tell him any of this, I swear," he said. "I just asked if he wanted to check out an old house."

"He didn't," Gilbert confirmed, and he settled back against the couch cushions with a smile. "I never want people to tell me what's going on in their homes. I insist on finding out myself." He cast his eyes around the room again, then settled his gaze on Deegie. "There's a lot going on in here. Interesting."

"It has been interesting, yes." His frosty blue eyes were a little unsettling, but only because they were so very much like her own. Deegie felt no ill will from him, but there was an odd sort of connection, a kinship almost.

"You should visit her shop someday," Zach put in. "Now *that's* interesting!" Even as he jested, Zach shivered: Deegie could tell he felt the presence of something else here.

"Get comfortable," Deegie said, "and I'll be back with tea. I have a bunch of herbal teas from the shop; I'll bring them out."

In the kitchen, she filled a basket with the teas and arranged slices of store-bought banana bread on a platter. When she turned to a cabinet to reach for the teacups, she wasn't at all surprised to see Gilbert, leaning against the door jamb and smiling his serene smile. "I'll help carry some of this for you," he said.

"Thank you. That would be nice." She handed him napkins and plastic forks and tried not to look at his eyes. "I really appreciate you coming here to check things out." She kept her tone casual and light; she was not quite ready to reveal her true self to him, although he was a witch just like she was. She'd felt it the minute he walked through the doorway.

"Hey, you can stop pretending you don't know what's going on," Gilbert said around a mouthful of banana bread.

"I don't know what you mean." She pretended to study her chipped red nail polish.

"Your parents told you to never tell anyone too, huh?" He picked up the basket of tea and tucked the napkins and plastic forks inside. His voice was casual, as if he's been chatting about the weather. "We natural-borns get that all the time. Did you make up your own names for spells when you were a kid? I sure did."

Deegie picked up the kettle and set it down again. She picked up an embroidered dishtowel and refolded it over the oven door handle, then gave up. There was really no point in denying it when they both knew what was going on. "Yes," she said, and ventured a laugh. "Yes, I sure did."

"We should compare notes sometime." Gilbert nudged open the kitchen door with his shoulder and paused. "But right now we have a unique set of ghostly circumstances to investigate, don't we?"

"Yes, we do." Relief and elation mixed and showed on her face; it had been so long since she'd met another like herself.

"Tea first," Gilbert said. "Come on!"

"Wait!" Deegie held up a hand and lowered her voice. "Does Zach know? About me, I mean."

"He told me he had his suspicions, but he wouldn't bring it up unless you did first. Said he could tell by your eyes. Magical people tend to have unusual eyes, didn't you know that?"

"Well, I—"

"Another thing we can chat about! Cool!" Gilbert shoved open the door again, and Deegie followed him out into the living room to rejoin Zach.

The three of them drank their tea and ate their banana bread, and finally Gilbert just came right out and said it: "So what's in the basement, Deegie?"

She was caught off-guard all over again, and her teacup and saucer jittered in her lap. "Oh! Well, it's, ah..." She sipped tea and tried again. "I found jars full of strange herbs. Stuff that...witches... rarely use anymore, poisonous stuff."

"What else, Deegie?" Zach leaned toward her encouragingly. "It's cool, I know what you are." He chuckled. "Why didn't you just tell me?"

She shrugged. "I already have the reputation for being the town weirdo. I don't usually tell people unless I'm very close to them. Spencer—my ex-boyfriend—he didn't even know. He just thought I liked the Goth look."

Bast awoke from his nap under the kitchen table and joined the trio of humans. He stalked across the coffee table, investigating cups and plates, then found Deegie's lap. He sat there, purring incessantly, and watched the conversation.

"There's something else in that basement though, Deegie. What else did you find? I can feel it, but you *saw* it." Gilbert reached out to pat Bast's tiny head as he asked his question.

"Fingers." said Deegie. "I found a jar with human fingers in it. I put it back on the table and got the hell out of there." She shredded the edge of her napkin as she spoke; her own agitated fingers needed something to do. "It looks to me like someone was trying to raise demons. It had to have been a long time ago though. Those jars are almost black with crud."

"We ran into Shit Storm Murphy the other night," Zach put in. "He was babbling on about a couple of brothers who rented rooms here and tried to raise a demon way back in the 1920s, then supposedly committed suicide. We thought he was just telling another one of his tall tales, you know how he is, then Deegie finds this stuff, and, well, maybe he wasn't fibbing this time."

"Really? Old Shit Storm's still alive? I'll be damned. I never heard anything bad about this old place, though. It's been sitting here boarded up since we were kids. It would be interesting to do a little research on it, though. Perhaps a trip to the library is in order." He scanned the room again, paying special attention to the high, pressed tin ceiling. "I don't feel any residuals from a suicide, though. Do you, Deegie?"

"No, but if what Murphy said is true, then the Underworld would have gobbled up their souls immediately. Demons love suicides." Her lips tightened in a forced smile. "But I'm sure you know that, right?"

"Hmm. Interesting concept. We'll go down there later and check it out. All three of us. Maybe all we need to do is throw all that crap away and give everything a good psychic scrubbing." Gilbert put his hands briefly to his forehead and drew in a deep breath. "Now then," he said. "The ghosts. A female, correct?"

"Yes. I've heard her voice. I've contacted her a couple of times."
Oh for crying out loud! she raged inwardly. *I finally get a chance to talk to another witch, and he turns out to be an uppity know-it-all!* She sat on her hands and made her face serene.

Gilbert nodded, and smiled with his eyes closed. "Yes, a woman. An older lady, and she's a little slow, isn't she? Mentally challenged, maybe. Sweet, though, and kinda timid."

"Yes, that's her. She has trouble communicating, but it never occurred to me that she might be, um, slow. Is she here?"

"Standing right over there by the door." Gilbert pointed in that direction. "She's looking at you, I think, and—oh! Cats! So many of them! I think it's safe to say that you have a ghostly crazy cat lady living here with you."

"Yeah, I think so too." Deegie said. "There's a pet cemetery in the backyard, as a matter of fact."

"I'd love to see it sometime." Gilbert made a dismissive gesture with his hands and stood up. "Now then. The basement. Tell me how you found those jars. It's important. Did you go down there of your own free will, or was something calling to you?"

Deegie lifted her chin, and she heard Zach snicker. She couldn't decide whether to be amused or annoyed by Gilbert's take-charge attitude; he reminded her of one of those motivational speakers who think they have all the answers. She admitted to him that she had indeed felt overwhelmingly compelled to find the key to the basement door, unlock it, and go shuffling down those stairs in her bunny slippers and explore the still, shadowy bowels of the house.

"Yes, I thought it was the cat lady, but when I got down there, I felt something else. Residual energy, maybe? It felt completely different than the energy from the lady and her cats. It was far from friendly. The second time I went down there—well, I really don't remember much about that. It was like...like sleepwalking. I'm not really sure what happened."

"Interesting. And yes, sleepwalking is one possibility." Gilbert extended his arm in the direction of the basement door. "Come on," he said. "Let's see what's down there."

The three of them headed down the hallway with Bast bringing up the rear. When they got to the door, Tiger Spirit rose up and blocked the way, his nebulous form rasping against the old wood. His jungle-like smell was thick and cloying.

Gilbert stumbled back a foot or two, as if he'd been pushed aside. "I see we've met your guardian," he said stiffly. "My parents never summoned one for me when I was a kid, but I sure wanted one. Tiger, right?"

"Yes, a Bengal. I call him Tiger Spirit. He doesn't want us to go downstairs."

The old four-panel door rattled against its frame as Tiger brushed past it again. A hot, damp cloud of his breath billowed out and warmed the space in front of them. Zach picked up Bast, backed up a few steps, then hurried back down the hallway, trailing his apology behind him. "Sorry, guys. I'm sitting this one out! Getting a little too weird for me!"

Gilbert looked like he wanted to laugh, but didn't quite make it. His freckled cheeks reddened and his voice lost a great deal of its former confidence. "Can you...call him off or something? Nothing will happen down there, I promise."

"I know that, but he obviously senses something or he wouldn't be doing this."

Deegie reached down and made stroking motions in the empty space between herself and the door. Her fingers found the ruff of fur around Tiger's neck, and she muttered soft words into his velvety ear, telling him she would be fine, that she was protected and would be right back. The grunting huff of the big feline receded down the hall a few paces, and the pressure in front of the door eased. Deegie and Gilbert switched on their flashlights and crept into the yawning black throat of the basement, and Tiger brought up the rear in a sinuous ripple of air.

The work table with its grim cargo appeared further away than it had on her first trip down here, and the back wall was canted somehow, sloping at an angle she hadn't noticed before. Tiger Spirit paced close to their legs as they drew closer, and a soft growl hovered in his throat. Deegie saw the blurred footprints her slippers had left behind the other night, saw the smudges her hands had left on the filthy jars.

"The one with the fingers is right in the middle," she said when they got to the edge of the table. "There are at least five of them in there. Didn't really stick around to count them once I realized what I was looking at."

"Can't blame you for that." Gilbert used his flashlight to spotlight the rows of mysterious jars. They reflected muted, sooty light, and exuded a graveyard chill. He picked up the jar with the most disturbing contents and held it in front of his face so he could examine the things inside. "Yup, those are fingers all right!"

"Put it down." Deegie patted the clean spot on the table where the jar had sat for so long. "Don't even touch that one." She slid another jar to the front of the table, the one bearing the label Roots of Both Hellebores. "Look. When was the last time you saw or even heard of herbs like this? This shit was used for raising demons, according to what my dad used to tell me. And look at this one." She slid another jar though the coating of dust on the table. "Black Henbane. Necromancers use this stuff!"

"Whoa. You weren't kidding, were you?" Gilbert reached out for the jars again, but she slapped his hands away.

Tiger Spirit paced anxiously, and he nudged repeatedly at the two witches. His great, unseen body scraped against the table, and the jars rattled together. The motion caused one of the dried fingers to roll away from its partners, and its yellowed nail clinked against the glass.

"I don't understand the fingers, though," said Gilbert. "The herbs, sure. Looks like someone was determined to raise a demon, or Ol' Scratch, or something, but why use fingers in the spell?"

"An offering, maybe?"

"Could be, could be." He crossed his arms over his chest and shivered extravagantly. "And you were right about the residual energies down here! Whoo! Brrr!"

The motivational speaker was back, arrogant and a trifle condescending. Deegie smiled anyway; he was irritating, yet charming in an odd sort of way. "Yeah, it's creepy," she agreed. "I don't feel any actual entities, though." She hesitated and added, "Do you?"

Gilbert scanned the room, one loosely curled hand raised to his chin in a pose that looked more affected than wise. "No, nothing."

"Okay then. Let's just find a box and start getting rid of this stuff. I'll probably never use this room for anything but storage, but I sure don't want these jars in here. Afterwards, we can smudge the place. I brought a couple of sage bundles, and I have plenty of salt."

* * *

Upstairs in the living room, Zach sat on the patchwork couch with Bast on his lap as he listened to the muffled voices of Deegie and Gilbert drift up through a vent on the wall. He could still hear the sound of Deegie's spirit guardian, that menacing *ungh, ungh, ungh* that a big cat makes just before a roar. He hadn't meant to run off like that, but Zach had never experienced anything like Tiger Spirit before. Not even being the only "normal" in a magical family had prepared him for that. He was a little embarrassed for running off, too. Now his brother was down in the basement with the girl he liked. Zach glared at the basement door and ran a gentle hand over the purring black kitten on his lap.

"What the heck's going on around here, kitty?" he asked, watching the little animal swat at his hands with its tiny paws. "Are there ghosts in here? Huh?"

Bast raised his head and eyed the kind human with the big red beard. His lap was a nice place to hang out for a while, but the tiny black kitten had important cat things to do, like finding out who was calling *here, kitty, kitty*...over by the stairs. Bast leaped off the human's lap and only stumbled a little when he landed. The voice called to him again, gently, hesitantly, and the black kitten homed in on its source. Just right over there, next to the kitchen doorway. It was one of those hazy, indistinct humans, the kind that looked like they were made from smoke. Oh, and a few of the smoke cats, too! Bast loved to play, and he didn't mind if his playmates were a little different. The smoke cats played a great game of hide-and-seek; sometimes they disappeared entirely!

Here, kitty, kitty...Come to Lisbet...

The human's outline wavered as she knelt down to stroke his fur.

Good kitty...won't hurt you...

CHAPTER SEVEN

WHEN THE LAST OF THE mysterious jars had been loaded into cardboard moving boxes, Gilbert carried them to the foot of the basement stairs, gallantly refusing to let Deegie help. Tiger Spirit grew increasingly restless, and he roamed the basement, huffing, grunting, and head-butting the humans to hurry them along.

"Can you make him stop?" Gilbert asked as he stumbled forward a few steps after a particularly insistent shove. "Why is he so agitated? There's nothing down here that's going to hurt you."

"He seems to think so," Deegie said. "I trust him; he's never been wrong. He wants us out of here, and I agree with him. Come on, let's go." She nudged the stack of boxes with the side of her foot. "I'll help you carry these upstairs."

Gilbert still held the jar of fingers in his hand, and he gave it a brisk shake. The shriveled digits clinked and rattled against the glass. "What about this one?" He wiped at the grime on the jar with the sleeve of his sweatshirt so he could have a better look at the contents. "You know, legally we need to report this to the police. They're human remains, technically."

Deegie considered this a moment, then shook her head. "No," she said. "I'll take the risk. All I want to do is get rid of them." She picked up the box on the top of the stack, grunted a little with the effort, then mounted the stairs. "Come on. Let's get this stuff out of here."

Gilbert shook the jar again, and Deegie whipped her head around to shoot him a withering glare. Chastised, he put the jar on top of the next box, picked it up, and followed her up the stairs. The box was heavy, and the jars inside made a brittle clanking noise as he made his way up the risers; the one with the fingers inside rolled dangerously close to the edge. Halfway to the top, the bottom of the box began to split. Gilbert brought a knee up to bolster the sagging cardboard flaps, but to no avail. Fourteen one-hundred-year-old jars fell through the open staircase and smashed on the concrete floor.

"Oh shit," Gilbert said mildly. "Sorry, Deegie. If you have a broom handy, I'll be happy to swee—"

An unearthly cry rose up from the litter of shattered glass and torn cardboard, and a cloud of ancient powdered herbs rose up along with it. Tiger Spirit shoved Gilbert to the top of the stairs with his mighty head, then replied to the eerie wail with a deafening roar. Gilbert pitched forward at the top of the stairs, and would have taken a nasty spill if Deegie hadn't caught him.

"What happened? What's going on?" Deegie scrambled to the doorway, dread rising in her throat. Gilbert grabbed her by the shoulders and spun her away from the entrance to the basement, but she squirmed out of his grasp and tried once more to go after her spirit guardian. "What was that? Let me see!" She made it over the threshold just as the basement light went out. Something huge and black, blacker than the darkened room itself, came boiling up the stairs, and Gilbert yanked her back again.

Like a mass of thick, polluted fog, the shadow thing loomed in the doorway. Long finger-like projections of blackish smoke shot out like whips, narrowly missing Deegie's head, and a mass of slit-pupiled eyes, dull orange and sickly, hung in the center like a cluster of diseased grapes. An acrid smell, like burning garbage, filled the hallway. Gilbert let go of Deegie's arm and streamed white light from his fingertips. The shadow thing howled, but did not retreat. It formed hands and gripped the doorframe while it shrieked at a white-faced Gilbert.

"Deegie, help me, damn it! Don't let it get out!" The voice of the younger Altman brother rose above the unearthly noise of the smoky horror as he unleashed another blast of protective light.

She wrenched her eyes away from the creature and raised both hands, knowing full well that the enormous amount of energy she was about to release would bring her equally enormous pain. The hellish cloud of black smoke roared at her as the back of the long hallway was illuminated by the double bolts of energy that shot out of Deegie's palms. The creature staggered back under the witches' combined forces, but not much, and Deegie realized she had been screaming for Tiger Spirit with both her voice and her mind.

Tiger had already heeded her call. He had been there all along, battling the thing from behind, trying unsuccessfully to pull it back down the staircase and into the gloomy recesses of the basement. Great clots of the thing's dark body were torn out by Tiger's claws and teeth, only to reattach themselves seconds later. With a sound like a sheet being torn in two, a hole opened up in the middle of the vaporous beast, right above its lidless eyes, and Tiger burst through in a shower of heat and brilliant gold sparks. Deegie felt the crackle of his energy as he landed between her and Gilbert, and the thunder of his roar shook the floorboards as he challenged the shadow thing to another round. The thing in the doorway pulled back, shrieking in rage as it tried to close the hole in its body. Deegie managed another burst of light and pushed it back even farther.

Gilbert slammed the door, and Deegie sank to her knees with her arms wrapped around her head. There was no grace period this time. The pain in her head came on hard and fast; there wasn't even time to make it to her bed or the couch to lie down. She was vaguely aware of Tiger standing guard at the door, and the indignant screech of the thing trapped in the basement sounded distant and foggy. Gilbert had a hand on her shoulder and was shaking her roughly, and from somewhere in the vast old house she heard Zach calling out her name, heard his pounding footsteps as he ran to her.

"What happened to her? Is she hurt?"

"There was—we had an accident," Gilbert said, panting for breath. "Apparently there was some sort of...entity...down there, and it's pretty pissed off at us. I've managed to contain it, and I should be able to—"

"What? What do you mean? What the hell did you do to her, you asshole?" Zach knelt by Deegie's side and brushed her wild black hair out of her eyes. "Deeg? You okay?"

"Nothing! I didn't do anything to her! She just fell after we fought off that thing down there!" Gilbert's face was ashen, and his tone was that of an indignant child. He stood up and wrung his hands as he looked down at Deegie.

She opened her mouth to assure the Altman brothers that she was uninjured, but she was preempted by another volley of enraged screeches and howls from the thing in the basement. She opened her eyes to slits and saw that Gilbert had sealed the door with a Locking Spell; fierce golden light filled the cracks around the edges, and she felt Tiger Spirit filling the space between her prone body and the basement door. She managed to rise to a sitting position, holding tightly to Zach's arms for support.

"I'm okay." Her voice wavered under the immense pressure in her head, and she extended an arm in the general direction of the basement. "There's something down there, Zach. Oh, shit, Murphy was right! It's worse than a ghost. It came up from the floor, right after the jars..." Her hands went to her head again, pressing tightly, and her eyes became huge and glassy in her face as a sudden realization clicked into place. "The jars broke. The one with the fingers..." She recalled the day she'd sat in the Bus outside the house, remembered the strange, disjointed words the gentle Lisbet had spoken when the two of them made contact: *The glass must not break...never break it...*

"There was something besides fingers in that jar, something horrible. When the jar broke, it got out. Black magic. I should have known."

The shadow thing roared and hissed in its basement prison, adding emphasis to Deegie's revelation.

"I didn't mean to," said Gilbert. "The box ripped. How was I to know that—"

"How about you shut up, and we take care of Deegie first?" Zach observed the way basement door shook and bowed out from its frame under the relentless blows of the demon on the other side. "Can that...that *thing* get out?"

"No. I used the Locking Spell, and Deegie's tiger guardian is here. It can't get out. I don't think so, anyway."

Zach helped Deegie to her feet, and when she stumbled, he scooped her up in his arms. "Come on, genius," he said, "let's get her to the couch."

Gilbert nodded, white-faced, and followed his brother into the living room.

Once she was stationed on the couch, wrapped in blankets, and given pain relievers, Deegie managed to explain her condition, although her teeth were still clenched in pain and her body was tense and trembling. "I'll be all right," she told the two of them in a voice barely above a whisper. "I get the worst headaches when I...when I use my abilities." She offered a weak smile of apology and felt more than a little embarrassed that her strange affliction had made itself known. "It happens sometimes with natural-born witches. I can only do a little magic at a time. It's called—"

"Witch's Cramp," Gilbert broke in. "It's rare among natural-borns. They can produce enormous amounts of energy, but it doesn't last long and causes the most awful headaches."

Deegie massaged her temples and said nothing.

"Witch's Cramp? I've never heard of it. Is there anything else I can do for you? God, you're so pale!" Zach wore a look of extreme distress and the racket from the dark creature in the basement certainly wasn't helping.

"No, no, I'll be fine, I just...I get real weak, and...it just hurts, that's all. It'll be a while before I can use my powers again, but I'm okay, Zach." Deegie hugged her legs and rested her pain-filled head on her knees. Trying to formulate a plan for what to do next was impossible right now, and all she really wanted was to be left alone until she was able to function again.

"Can you kill that thing or something? Make it go back to Hades, or wherever it came from?" Zach shrugged, palms up. "I'm sorry if that sounds stupid. I just...I just don't understand how this works. I'm the normal one here, remember."

"I have absolutely no idea," Gilbert admitted, and he got up and went to the window to stare glumly out at the night.

Deegie grimaced and massaged her temples. "Guys, just shut up a sec, okay? I can't think right now. Ugh! My damn head!"

Zach's hand hesitated over Deegie's head, then dropped to his side. "Let's go in the other room for a few minutes," he said to Gilbert. To Deegie, he said, "We're not leaving you here by yourself tonight, you know."

Once the room was quiet–save for the incessant low growling of the basement demon from the floor below–Deegie was able to relax her overtaxed body by slow degrees, and the agonizing pressure in her head lessened. Only then was she able to replay the situation in her mind and decide what to do next. *I have a demon in my basement.* If it had been happening on TV or in a book, she would have laughed at the ridiculousness of it all. At least no one was hurt–or worse. Tiger Spirit had blocked the entire end of the hall, and she heard his panting breath from across the house. Zach and Gilbert were safe too; she heard the quiet murmur of their voices in the next room, and Bast was...

"Bast?" Deegie tossed aside the blankets and sat up. *Where was Bast?* "Kitty, kitty? Oh no, please don't let him be in the basement..."

CHAPTER EIGHT

"BAST! WHERE ARE YOU? KITTY, kitty?" Deegie sprang from the couch, the blanket draped around her shoulders like a cape, and ran to the living room door on legs that still wobbled. A woman's voice, singing, stopped her in the doorway. Deegie recognized it at once as the song she'd heard the night before, only this time it was bold, and clear, and beautiful: The Flower Duet from Delibes' *Lakmé*.

"Lisbet? Is that you?" Deegie called out uncertainly. "Please talk to me. I need your help."

Mew!

The mew of a kitten, strident and insistent, rose above the ghostly soprano voice, and tears of relief stung Deegie's eyes as she saw a fuzzy black shape dashing down the hallway towards her.

"Bast! Oh, thank all the gods!" She bent over to pick him up, but he dashed away from her and jumped up on the couch she'd recently vacated.

The kitten gave one of his paws a perfunctory lick, then opened his mouth. The next line from *Lakmé* flowed over the tiny pink tongue and Deegie almost screamed. Impossibly, incredibly, Bast was singing while he swatted at the tassels on the throw pillows.

Deegie grabbed him and folded him in her arms. "Lisbet! Are you doing this to him? Stop it! Don't you dare hurt him!"

"Not hurt! Never hurt kitties!" The reply came from the purring ball of fur in her arms.

Bast looked up at her calmly and reached for her hair with a questing paw. *"We all sing together. Never any hurt. Sorry...sorry..."*

"Lisbet? Wh-what are you doing? Are you...in my cat's body?"

Lisbet giggled, and Bast's constant purr made it come out shivery. *"Fun...such fun...the Tiger doesn't know. I could not pass by him, so I hide...here! Kitten takes me to you...speak to you and see you now!"*

Deegie sat again, and Bast jumped from her lap and attacked a forgotten dust ball in the corner of the room. Being momentarily possessed by a soprano-voiced ghost didn't seem to be a problem for him; the black kitten was just as curious and playful as ever.

"Lisbet, what's happening here? What is that thing in the basement? Do you know?"

A long sigh of utter despair emanated from Bast as he playfully chased his tail; the contrast between voice and action was downright eerie, even for Deegie.

"Bad things! Bad! The glass...it has broken. The men..."

"Gilbert didn't mean to break it," Deegie said patiently. "I know something was released when that jar of fingers broke. I need you to tell me everything you know about it so I can fix it."

"Please don't send me away..."

Deegie's heart clenched, and her throat tightened. "No, Lisbet. I won't send you away. I want you to stay here with me, you and all your kitties. But I need to get rid of the evil in here first so we can be happy. Do you understand?"

Lisbet sighed again. Bast pounced on Deegie's foot.

"Lisbet? Can you answer me? Tell me what you know. Please."

"Eighteen-eighty three! Right here in this house, me...born HERE!"

Deegie closed her eyes and breathed in calming pink light. This was going to take a while. The long-dead lady was a gentle soul, but Gilbert had been correct: she was a bit slow.

"Did you live in this house all your life?"

"Yes, yes...mother, father, brother. All gone...only me now. We all sing together...Christmas..."

"You must have had some wonderful Christmases here, Lisbet." Deegie got to her feet and captured Bast before he ran out the door and took the ghost with him. Bast purred and squirmed and batted at her nose. "When it is time for Christmas, I will decorate this house just for you, if you can tell me who put the jars in the basement." Deegie did not observe Christmas herself, but she did enjoy the look of a house dressed up in winter finery.

"In the basement. Oh, it is loose! The glass must not break! It must not! My hand!"

Lisbet's voice was edged in panic now, and Deegie immediately regretted upsetting the childlike soul. Whatever happened in this house had obviously been traumatizing for her.

"Shhh, it's okay, Lisbet. Don't be frightened; I won't let anything hurt you, I promise." A thought occurred to her then, a wholly unpleasant one. "Lisbet, these bad men, did they...did they hurt you? Did they do a bad thing to you?"

She received no reply for several long moments. Bast dragged his claws trough her wild black curls and bit her nose, completely oblivious to the sad ghost playing stowaway in his body.

"I rent out the house when I am old. Rooms for rent...bad men came. Oh, bad, bad...Fingers all bloody...they make a book, it hides in the wall...like me..."

And with that, Lisbet left Bast's body; Deegie felt her go. Bast wriggled in her grasp, wanting to be put down, so she let him have his way. He bounced across the couch cushions, eager to begin a new adventure. Deegie sensed that Lisbet was still near, hovering near the ceiling, but at the sound of the brothers' approaching footsteps, she passed through the layers of paint, and plaster, and wood beams, and hid herself away on the second floor.

Those men killed her, Deegie thought. *I'd be willing to bet they did. Bastards.*

Zach poked his head into the room. "Deeg? Who are you talking to in here?"

"Bast," she said. "Only it wasn't Bast, it was someone else."

"Well, that makes tons of sense." He sat beside her. "You feeling any better?"

"Aside from the pissed-off ball of growling smoke in my basement and the ghost of a crazy cat lady taking over my kitten's body, I'm just dandy."

"Wait—what? Are you serious? Is he okay?" Zach was alarmed; he had clearly developed quite a fondness for little Bast.

"Yes, he's just fine. Didn't faze him a bit. Lisbet couldn't get past Tiger, so she hitched a ride inside Bast."

"Holy crap. That's amazing!" Zach looked around the room. "Is she...here?"

"No. She got upset and left. I was able to ask a few questions, but it's hard to understand her. She knows what happened here, and she knows who put the jars in the basement." Deegie grimaced and massaged her temples. "I will try to talk to her again later."

Gilbert entered the room, looking dejected and humble as he gnawed on a thumbnail. The bizarre events of the evening had robbed him of his cockiness. "The door's still holding up," he announced. "I can still hear that thing fumbling around down there, but at least it's quieter now." He glanced at the empty spot on the couch next to Deegie, but remained standing.

"Thank you, Gilbert," she said, feeling a little sorry for him. Although she knew he'd most likely been listening in on her conversation with Zach, she let him in on what had just happened to her and Bast.

Gilbert stroked Bast's fur as he listened, and he didn't interrupt this time. "I can help if you want," he said when she'd finished. "I have contacted ghosts before and communicated with them."

"I get the feeling she's afraid of men. Poor soul. Thanks Gilbert, but I think I should be the one to talk to Lisbet. She's very fragile, and this is going to require a gentler touch," Deegie said. "She said something about 'bad men' who came, and hid a book in a wall."

"Book of Shadows, maybe?" Zach asked. "I know what those are, at least."

"Yes, I think that's what she meant, but I'm going to see if I can get more information from her before we start ripping out walls." She yawned hugely and rubbed her reddened eyes. "Guys, if you don't mind, I think I'm going to try to get a little sleep now."

"Here?" Gilbert was incredulous. "Not here, you're not! Are you kidding?" He looked over at Zach hopefully. "Right Zach?"

"Absolutely not." Zach stood and tugged at Deegie's arm. "We have a guest room where you can stay until this house is safe again. Pack a bag, grab Bast, and let's go. You need rest, and you're not gonna get it here, that's for sure!"

Deegie knew better than to argue; she was outnumbered, and they were right. It would be foolish to stay here.

* * *

Jarvis "Shit Storm" Murphy could sleep just about anywhere as long as the weather was warm, and he did so quite often. Whenever happy hour at the Cantina or the Shady Inn got a little too out of hand, and he didn't want to risk another DUI, Murphy would go to one of many little hide-outs in the woods and sleep it off until he was sober enough to drive home. Several of these hidey-holes had been in use for years, some of them even dating back to his father's time, when the old man used to hide from his Temperance Union wife.

Now that the cold weather was moving in, the forest hide-outs were no longer cozy wooded refuges from a sober world; Murphy had frozen his ass off last night, and he reluctantly decided as he crawled out from under pine boughs and chunks of sheltering bark that this would have to be the last night in the woods until spring. Shivering in the pink light of dawn, he stood and had a good full-body scratch while he got his bearings and tried to remember where he had parked his truck. Snow was in the air; he could feel it. If his memory served him correctly, there should still be a bottle of Night Train back home, under the kitchen sink next to the floor bucket. It would serve double duty, both as breakfast and to take the chill from his rapidly aging bones.

Just through the trees and down the hill stood the newly inhabited 14 Fox Lane: the creaky old barn purchased by the young lady he'd spoken to last night. Sheltered by lofty pines and with a dusting of frost across the roof shingles, it fairly glowed with its fresh coat of white paint, and its newly cleaned windows reflected chilly morning sunshine. If he took the barely discernable path through the trees that ran alongside the house and down to the street, he might be lucky enough to catch a glimpse of the raven-haired lady of the house and apologize again for his behavior the other night. *Was it last night, or the night before?* he wondered as he started down the hill, *and what exactly did I say to her? Damn tequila. Always stealing away good memories. Or was that gin?*

As he came closer to the house, Murphy noticed that the young lady's *(Debbie? Diane? Something with a D)* colorfully painted van was missing from the driveway once again. She didn't seem to stay around much. Then he remembered the red-haired kid from the Cantina who'd been with her that night. *I betcha that's where she is! Keepin' warm with her beau!* Murphy's phlegmy cackle startled a couple of jays from their roost in the branches above, and they flew, scolding and cawing, into the sunrise. The carpet of pine needles, soon to be covered by winter snow, crunched under his feet. He touched the tough new skin of paint on the old boards and wondered if he should take a quick peek in one of the windows, just to see what else she'd done with the place. *I bet everything's all pink and girly, with ribbons and bows, and—*"

From somewhere deep in the house, a woman screamed.

Murphy backpedaled, tripped over a fallen branch, landed on his ass, and bit his tongue. She was home after all! And, judging by what he had just heard, she was in a powerful heap of trouble, as his dearly departed daddy used to say.

Another scream, louder and more insistent, tore from the lower half of the house. *Locked in the basement, maybe? Somebody hurting her?*

Goddamn it, this isn't what I had on the agenda for today! Murphy hustled to the back of the house, where two boarded-up windows nestled close to the ground. Another scream filtered through the splintery boards, and Murphy knelt in frozen mud to wedge a couple of his beefy fingers around the weakest looking board. "Hold on, dammit! Just hold on!" he yelled to the distraught woman inside. The board came free with a single yank; the exposed window glass was black and opaque, as if it had been spray-painted. A lacy net of spider webs swayed in the corners.

"You in there? Hey, lady! What's wrong with you? You okay in there?" He put his lips close to the filthy glass, hoping his voice would project better to the woman trapped inside. The last of his leftover tequila buzz vanished and Shit Storm Murphy found himself horribly sober. He pulled away from the window and got his fingers behind the second board, ready to yank it free and break through the glass. From behind the filmy windowpane came a stealthy, scuttling noise, like someone rushing towards him through a pile of leaves. Something tapped on the glass, and Murphy hoped to hell it was the woman he was clumsily attempting to rescue. "Hang on, lady! Almost there!" He heaved backwards on the weather-beaten board, and the squeal of wood against nails coincided with another peal of anguish from the other side of the window. The tap turned into a loud bang, and the glass shivered in its frame as something was pressed against it.

A face, horrid and squashed-looking, peered out at him with a cluster of lidless, jack o' lantern eyes. A mouth widened in a drooling crescent lined with crooked, rotting teeth, and it screamed again, a perfect imitation of a woman in distress.

Murphy spun away from the window, his face distorted in a terrified grimace, and he headed for the woods in a shambling run. He wasn't built for speed and some days he could barely walk, but he forced his legs to keep moving anyway, taking him back up the hill and deeper into the woods. "It's them demons, them demons..." The words ripped from his mouth in clouds of steam, and his heart sledgehammered dangerously in his chest. The only demons he'd experienced before were the ones that came out of a whiskey bottle. He located his lean-to of bark and branches and dove into it, getting dirt up his nose and pine needles down his shirt. Murphy huddled in the early morning cold, praying to whatever gods would listen and pressing his hands hard against the bomb going off in his chest.

* * *

She grew tired of staring at the ceiling, so she turned on her side in the narrow twin bed and stared at the wall instead. Bast purred in his sleep next to her pillow, and the wind-up alarm clock counted down the seconds remaining until sunrise. Deegie gave up and got out of bed. The enticing smell of brewing coffee cut through the bachelor-pad aromas of neglected laundry piles and leftover pizza, and she left the cluttered guest room to find the source. Zach stood in the kitchen, scratching at his red beard and frowning at the instructions on a box of pancake mix.

"Morning," she mumbled. "Need help with that?"

"Deeg!" He put down the pancake mix and gave her an awkward, one-armed hug. "Did you sleep okay? Oh, and I forgot to apologize for the mess in here last night. Just, you know, the whole 'guys are slobs' thing."

"Pour me some of that coffee, and you'll be forgiven."

"Yes, ma'am." Zach poured coffee in a huge yellow mug, set it in front of Deegie, and watched her take a sip. "Well, you're not gagging. Must be okay to drink, then."

Her lips twitched in a suggestion of a smile, but she said nothing and sipped from the mug again.

"Hey, you okay? Sorry, dumb question. Of course you're not." He looked at the pancake mix again, embarrassed.

"I'll be fine," she said automatically. Her tone indicated that she was nowhere close to being fine, but further discussion on the subject was closed. "Where's Gilbert?"

"Asleep, I think. Hey, Deeg, I'm sorry about him. He's a little—"

"Sure of himself? I noticed."

"Not so much anymore. Whatever's going on in your house humbled him in a fast hurry."

"I noticed that, too." Deegie took a few more swallows from the yellow mug, then set it down. "I should go," she said. "Thanks for letting me stay here last night." She scooped up Bast with one hand and grabbed her purse with the other.

"Wait, you're not going back there, are you?" Zach put down the pancake mix and followed her to the door.

"No." She smiled to cover her lie. "I have a lot of work to do at The Silent Cat before I open today. Shipments to put away, more stuff to order, that sort of thing. Life's gotta go on, you know. With or without basement demons."

CHAPTER NINE

A HARD FREEZE HAD GRIPPED Fiddlehead Creek during the night, and the roads were treacherous with patches of ice. Deegie made the trip from the Altman brothers' house to her own at a sedate twenty-five miles per hour, but there was still plenty of time before she had to open the shop. She brought her car to a stop across the street from the house, just as she'd done a few days before, and sat there for a minute, engine idling, before turning into the driveway. Bast was in the back of the Bus, exploring and content with his own small affairs, and Deegie decided he would be better off if she left him there this time. Lisbet hadn't hurt him in the slightest when she'd borrowed his body to talk to Deegie, but the idea of hearing her pet singing an aria again was just too creepy, even for her. "Stay here, little guy," she told the kitten. "I'll be back in just a few minutes."

The howling began when she unlocked the door and stepped into the foyer: the demon in the basement was awake, aware, and extremely pissed off. The long hallway seemed darker than usual, as if lined with living shadows. The basement door still glowed around the cracks; Gilbert's Locking Spell was still in place. Tiger Spirit was still here too. She felt his presence, and could smell his jungle scent. She dropped to her knees by the spot where he lay and dug her fingers into his thick coat. The demon roared and screamed, infuriated by its imprisonment, but Deegie felt safe and at ease in the presence of her guardian.

As Deegie had expected, a misty, tattered shadow appeared at the foot of the staircase and rippled like a heat wave. Other shadows, smaller and without discernable shape, glided down the banisters and risers to pool around the larger one, and Deegie heard the mews and purrs of a dozen cats. Lisbet and her companions came no closer; they were fully aware of Tiger's presence. The magnificent unseen guardian saw them too, and his warning growl was ominous. "It's okay, Tiger. They won't hurt me," Deegie soothed the huge invisible beast. She felt him relax then, but not much.

"Bad things in my house," Lisbet whispered sadly. *"I can still fear... fear for you."*

"Don't worry, Lisbet. I will make that bad thing go away, and then we can all be happy here. I promise."

"Bad things...bad, bad, things...oh, it's here, it's here..."

"Sssh, I know, I know. Don't worry; everything will be all right. My friends and I will get rid of the bad things." She kept her tone low, her voice soothing, as if she were talking to a small, frightened child. "Lisbet, do you remember the book you told me about? The one the bad men wrote? Do you remember what wall they hid it in?"

"Men are bad...the fingers...blood..."

"Lisbet, the bad men are gone now. My friends are *good* men, and they are going to help me get rid of the bad thing in the basement, but we need to find the book you told me about. Do you understand?"

"Witches...witches...are you bad?"

"No, Lisbet. You know I'm not. I'm your friend."

"Ah...? Kitty-kitty?"

"Bast isn't here right now, but you can play with him soon. The book, Lisbet. Where did the bad men hide the Book of Shadows?"

"Books...so many books. Cooking from a book!" Lisbet giggled, switching gears now. Her misty shape wavered on the gloomy

staircase, and the ghost cats tumbled and played around her, looking for all the world like large, indistinct dust balls.

Deegie pulled in a deep breath for patience and tightened her fingers in Tiger's fur. "The bad men's book, Lisbet. Please tell me where it is."

"We cook from a book...mother...sister...kitchen...holiday dinner on Christmas! So warm the house...tree...gifts..."

"That sounds like wonderful fun, Lisbet," Deegie said, and she meant it. Although she'd never participated in the Christmas holiday, she'd always been fascinated by it. Every year she felt the warm glow of love and camaraderie emanating from the Normal Ones, and she had always promised herself that she would try Christmas for herself someday. "I can make Christmas for you, Lisbet. I promise. I just need your help first, okay sweetie?"

Lisbet's misty form wavered again, and, just for a moment, she manifested fully. She was tiny and plump, with a long grey braid, her eyes framed with nets of fine lines. She was dressed in the clothing style of her day, and in one hand she cradled a tiny kitten. Her other hand was tucked deep into the pocket of her long apron.

"They put me in the garden...with the kitties..."

Her little form wavered, like windblown cobwebs, and the gentle spirit tucked her hand deeper into her apron pocket, then nuzzled the ghostly kitten in her other hand and sighed. The sound was heart-wrenching.

"Who put you in the garden, Lisbet? Do you mean the pet cemetery? Did someone...did the bad men bury you there? Is that what happened? Please tell me. If...if your bones are in the garden, I can...I can move them for you. I can give you a real burial in a real cemetery."

"No! Don't send me away! You promised! With the kitties...always with the kitties...by the bird bath. I am by the bird bath. Want to stay here...with you..."

Deegie's cell phone bleated from deep in the pocket of her coat, and the timid Lisbet vanished immediately at the unexpected sound. Deegie muttered mild curses and checked the caller ID. When she saw Zach's number she answered, getting to her feet. He started speaking before she could finish saying hello.

"Deeg, I'm sitting here in the parking lot of your shop and wondering why you're not here. Why is it that I have a feeling you're back at the house, roaming around and talking to ghosts?"

"Zach, I'm safe, I promise you. That thing can't get out, and if it does, Tiger will kick its ass. Listen, I'm trying to communicate with Lisbet. She knows where that book is, but it's hell trying to make sense out of what she says. And Zach, I think those brothers killed her, I really do. She said something about being put in the garden with the kitties."

"That's awful. Those bastards. Is she...there right now?"

"She was. The phone scared her off. She's like a frightened deer or something, poor thing. Oh well, I'll try later."

"You should at least take Gilbert with you next time."

"Umm, no. No, I can handle it. I'm perfectly safe, don't worry." She pulled back the cuff of her glove to check her watch. "Hey, gotta go. I'm going to be late."

She hung up before he could protest any further.

Deegie went around to the back of the house. The frozen grass made a brittle crunching sound under her feet, and the dead rosebushes sparkled with frost, but she hardly noticed the cold. In her eagerness to explore the area around the pink marble birdbath, she didn't even notice the square piece of plywood lying on the frozen ground next to the basement window. The makeshift tombstones of the pet cemetery were lacy with frost too, making them look all the more heartbreaking.

The area just behind the birdbath had not yet been cleared of brambles and debris, but Deegie clearly saw a sunken spot where the earth had settled after so many years. This was the only indication that a body had been buried here; there was no marker, not even a rough approximation of one. The woman who had built the tiny cemetery as a loving monument to decades of deceased cats had only dead pine needles and rotting vegetation to mark her final resting place. The irony was heartbreaking.

* * *

After spending most of the day dusting shelves and racking her brain for everything she knew about demons, Deegie decided to call it a day and hung up her ornately-lettered CLOSED sign. Snow had begun falling a few hours earlier, the flakes huge and downy, and the roads were becoming increasingly treacherous. It was best to get home—or in this case, back to the Altman brothers' house—before the weather got any worse. Besides, she'd only had one customer since she'd opened. As she gathered up Bast and her cavernous purse, she thought how wonderful it would be to sprawl out on her own bed in her own room with a new magazine and a cup of tomato soup. But little luxuries like that would have to wait; she had a slight demon problem to contend with first. Tonight she would confer with Gilbert, but Deegie could not resist another trip to her own house first, both to contact Lisbet again, and to check on Tiger Spirit. It felt bizarre driving down the street, past all the shops and houses full of people who went on about their lives without a single clue of the horror that lay, trapped and furious, in a basement just down the road.

What if it gets out? The distressing thought tried to surface, but Deegie pushed it back down; negative thoughts bred like flies, and she refused to acknowledge their presence.

The Bus skidded alarmingly to the left as she navigated the turn into her driveway, causing a few seconds of throat-tightening panic, and she reminded herself to have the snow tires put on first thing tomorrow. This would have to be a short visit. The way the snow was piling up, she'd be stuck in a snowdrift if she didn't get back to the Altmans' place soon.

The bellowing of the captive demon was the first thing she heard when she got out of the car. It came up through the ground, filtered and muffled by the soil and the stone foundation of the basement, and the blades of frozen grass fairly vibrated under Deegie's feet. Faintly, from the second floor, she heard Lisbet's whispery, hysterical voice: *"It knows...it must not...must not..."*

Deegie ran through the snow to the front door. She slipped once going up the front steps and almost went to her knees on the splintery porch. A whispered prayer slipped from her lips in a steamy ribbon as she plunged the house key into the old-fashioned lock and turned the knob. *Please don't let it be out! It can't get out, Tiger won't let it get out!* But she didn't hear Tiger. She heard the muted screams of the demon, certainly, and the frightened, wispy voice of Lisbet, hiding on the second floor, but where was Tiger's familiar husky rumble and comforting grunt?

She dashed down the hallway without bothering to shut the door, and her footsteps echoed throughout the dark, freezing house. From under the floor, the demon tracked her progress, pounding on the floorboards in time to her footfalls. A tendril of black, reeking smoke issued forth from a floor vent and humped across a throw rug in pursuit of Deegie's ankle. Her hand went up instinctively, and she vaporized the intruder with a short burst of light. The demon shrieked in outrage, and the floorboards rattled and bowed under its violent blows. Her wet boots betrayed her, and slid the last few feet to the basement door to collide with Tiger, who was still at his post.

"Tiger! What's wrong? What happened?" Her hands sought out the ruff of fur around the great guardian's neck, and she fairly cried out with relief when she felt his hot, panting breath against her hands. The air in front of the door rippled as he raised his great head and roared his reply to the screeching nightmare in the basement. Tiger was weakening: he'd spent too much time in the physical world, had expended too much energy protecting his human charge from the unwholesome thing that had been birthed from a jar of fingers. Another dark spiral of smoke shot out from under the door and snatched greedily at Tiger's vague shape, and the golden light of Gilbert's Locking Spell began to crumble along the top. Dying copper embers of the once-powerful spell spiraled down to leave pinpoint burn marks on the floor. It was getting out. Even worse, its writhing, root-like appendages were tearing chunks out of Tiger, stealing his energy and growing stronger.

Deegie scrambled to her feet and screamed out the words of the Locking Spell: *"Cincinno Lucis!"* Brilliant gold light streamed from her hands and filled the cracks of the door to overflowing. The excess oozed out in golden rivulets to puddle on the floor around Tiger. The old wooden door and its frame took on a fiery glow, and the odor of charred wood filled the hallway as the entry to the basement was resealed. The questing tentacle exploded in a shower of white sparks as it was sheared from the rest of the demon's body, and the evil creature shrieked in protest as it was forced to retreat.

Deegie collapsed on the floor next to Tiger and sent the rest of her energy directly into her guardian's ethereal body. The excess energy from the Locking Spell was absorbed as well, and Tiger's roar of triumph silenced the indignant wails of the captive demon—for now. Sprawled on the floor, Deegie smiled even as she struggled for breath. She couldn't wait to see the look on that know-it-all Gilbert's face when she told him about this! But a full-fledged gloating session would have to wait. Already she felt the tightening of her scalp, and the bee-sting tingling at the base of her neck: the after-spell dynamite was about to go off in her head. Her hands scrabbled for her purse before she realized she didn't have it. She'd left it, along with the bottle of pain relievers inside, under the passenger seat in the Bus.

She go to her feet, hoping she'd left the new bottle in the kitchen and not at Zach's place. The charred wood smell from the basement door made her stomach flip over and her heart hammered at a terrible pace as she stumbled to the kitchen. Tiger stayed where he was, but Deegie was reassured by his renewed strength; her own would return soon enough. The bottle of migraine pills, brand new and still in its box, sat on the narrow kitchen counter next to the pepper mill, and she nearly sobbed with relief when she saw it. She tore through the packaging and chewed three tablets, wincing at the bitter taste. Her quivering hands managed to snag a bottle of spring water out of the refrigerator, and she collapsed onto a kitchen chair to wait out the worst of the Witch's Cramp.

When she was able to grip the bottle hard enough to open it, Deegie gulped down enough water to rinse away at least some of the pain pills' awful taste. She supposed it was hell on her teeth, but chewing the pills had always brought her the fastest relief. As she sipped cold water and concentrated on her breathing, she felt the unmistakable presence of Lisbet, hovering in the kitchen doorway, felt the peculiar *click* in her mind as the ghost initiated contact.

"Safe...?"

Deegie grimaced in pain as she attempted to reply; if she forced it, she might manage a few words. "Yes, we are safe. The book... where...?"

There was no reply from Lisbet, but Deegie felt light, sudden pressure on her lap, and in her ear was the wonderfully soothing sound of a cat's purr. "Bast...?" With her eyes still clamped shut, she reached out for the source of the purring, and her questing hand encountered a mass of warm air that made her fingers tingle. She knew what it was at once: she was stroking the fur of one of Lisbet's ghostly feline companions. A silky warmth wrapped around her ankles as another of the spirit cats offered comfort, while the one on her lap made gentle kneading motions on her leg with its wispy paws. A chorus of purrs rumbled around her now, and a long fluffy tail brushed against her ankles.

"Good kitties..." Lisbet spoke at last, her dainty voice as soothing as the purrs of the ghostly cats. *"My magic...cat magic."*

"Yes, cat magic is good magic." The tightness in her head lessened under the soothing ministrations of the four-legged ghosts, and Deegie straightened in her chair. "Thank you, Lisbet. How did you do that?"

Lisbet giggled and said nothing.

"Oh, it's a secret, is it? Okay, you don't have to tell. Can you tell me where the book is, though? Is that okay?"

The purrs of the cats faded into the kitchen wall; Deegie heard the patting of their tiny pads against the floor until they stopped near the refrigerator. Lisbet said nothing.

"Lisbet? Can you hear me?"

Something rustled on top of the refrigerator, and a bag of chips she'd placed there earlier slid over to the edge, then dropped over the side, missing Bast's water bowl by mere inches.

She went to the refrigerator and knelt to pick up the fallen bag of chips. The floor creaked alarmingly and a small section of it sank beneath her foot. She leaped backwards, still clutching the chips, and the floor sprang back up again. An idea came to her like a thunderclap, and she knelt down again to administer a series of experimental raps to the left and right of the sagging floor board. When she rapped her knuckles across the center, the hollow sound was unmistakable: there was an empty space under the floor.

Deegie fumbled around in the cabinet beneath the sink until she found a putty knife, then returned to the hollow spot in the floor and wedged the blade under the edge of a square of linoleum. "Did you mean the *floor*, Lisbet?" she asked as she loosened old adhesive. "Is the bad men's book in the floor and not the wall?"

Lisbet didn't reply, and when Deegie looked up, she realized that the shy little ghost had gone. "Thank you, Lisbet. I'll make a beautiful Christmas for you, I promise," Deegie said to her anyway as she wielded the putty knife against the stubborn linoleum. A section of it loosened and cracked in half, and she tossed it aside to examine the floorboards underneath. The exposed wood was a darker color than the rest of the flooring, and there was a perfectly round hole in the center of it, just big enough for someone to insert a fingertip and pull that section out. The rest of the false floorboard was still held fast by the generous applications of adhesive and layers of linoleum, but she knew what she had found.

She got a flashlight from the utility drawer and shone its yellow circle of light down into the hole. All she saw was a piece of rough brown cloth, like burlap, and the dried body of a long-dead spider, but she knew the Book of Shadows was in here too. Lisbet had been confused as to which word to use, but she had known exactly where it was, just as Deegie had suspected.

When she stood up the room canted oddly to the left, and her first thought was that her excavation had somehow caused the entire floor to collapse. Instinctively, her hands shot out for the edge of the table to brace herself, but she remained upright; the floor was level once more. The sensation left her with a sickening vertigo, and she managed a muttered, "What the hell...?" before the room banked to the right this time, and she grabbed madly for the table again.

Beneath her feet, separated by mere inches of wood and horse-hair insulation, she heard the demon chuckle, as though he were pleased to discover that he could still manipulate the humans even if he couldn't escape from his basement prison.

"Knock it off, you jackass!" Deegie gripped the back of the chair and the edge of the wainscoting, readying herself for another ride on the demon-go-round. She wasn't sure how the foul creature was managing to play with her mind from the confines of the basement, but she wasn't about to let it think that it was winning. The floor bucked and heaved. Deegie heard the creaking of the old wood as it strained against the square-cut nails. Although she was nearly knocked off her feet again, she knew it wasn't real, and wondered how long she could put up with the demon's ruse. She had wanted a house like this her entire life; giving up wasn't an option.

The illusions continued, and became even more mind-bendingly realistic. The battery-operated clock on the wall melted and dripped in long yellow runnels, and the teakettle on the stove flapped its spout cover and clucked like a chicken. The room did another crazy, funhouse spin and the walls themselves began to run and distort as though they were made of hot taffy.

"Nice try!" Deegie yelled. "Is that the best you can do, you second rate-demon? Pssh! I wear heels bigger than your balls!" She had no idea if there was any risk involved when it came to provoking a captive demon, but she was beyond caring. "You're going to have to do better than that if you're trying to scare me out of *my* house!" She braced her feet and prepared for another onslaught, reminding herself over and over that this wasn't real, wasn't happening except in her head.

The new stove and refrigerator became animated lumps of white enamel and chrome, which tore themselves away from the walls with horrendous wrenching sounds and trundled across the kitchen. The refrigerator's door was now an obscenely flapping mouth that vomited groceries. Apples and oranges rolled across the floor, shrieking with tiny, toothless mouths, and the chicken she'd bought to make stew tumbled into a puddle of soy milk, tore free from its plastic bag, and flailed its naked limbs. It flipped over onto its breast and crawled towards Deegie with erratic jerks of its plucked wings and naked, truncated legs. Waves of nausea rushed her from all sides as a foul, open-sewer stench poured into the kitchen from a heating vent. She gagged and fought to control her gorge over this latest assault to her senses. The chicken dragged itself closer and reached out for her shoe with a questing wing tip.

"Nice sideshow, death breath." Her voice dripped with scorn, but her heart was galloping crazily in her chest, and her breathing was quick and shallow, as if the air were scarce. As much as she hated to admit it to herself, the demon's mind-bending antics were becoming too much to bear. She kicked the creeping chicken and sent it hurtling into the kitchen sink, where it flopped and writhed and emitted thick, burping noises from its empty body cavity. "You bore me, but I'll be back. You can be sure of that!"

Hoping that her fear didn't show through her false bravado, she left the house and walked out into the plum-colored twilight. Once she ascertained that Bast was still warm and safe in his cozy nest on the cot, she started the Bus and made the cautious drive through the blizzard back to the Altman house.

CHAPTER TEN

WITH ZACH'S SWEATSHIRT DRAPED OVER her shoulders and a mug of hot chocolate and peppermint schnapps in her hand, Deegie told the wide-eyed Altman brothers of her latest adventures in her extremely haunted house. "The Book of Shadows is under the floorboards; I just know it is. Lisbet gets confused with her words, so she knocked that bag of chips down to show me where to look." She pointed at the open bag, which now sat on the coffee table, then stuffed a couple of the chips into her mouth. "I need you guys to help me pry up part of the kitchen floor so we can get it out, though. We can go just as soon as I refuel."

Gilbert turned away from the window where he had been watching the snow fall. "You don't mean *tonight*, I hope. You need rest; you're far from full capacity—such as it is—and we're in the middle of a blizzard, in case you haven't noticed." He held the curtain open and moved aside so she could see for herself.

Pointedly ignoring his subtle insult, she sipped from her mug and observed the fat, feathery flakes which had been falling on and off all day. "Zach has a Jeep," she said, "with four-wheel drive. Plus he has snow chains."

"Deeg, I think Gil's right," Zach said, motioning for his brother to close the curtains. "Everything is secure at the house, you said so yourself. It can wait another night." He leaned over and poured another splash of peppermint schnapps into her mug. "Think about yourself for once and get some rest. I'm sure the ghost will understand."

"Tiger's getting weak," she reminded the brothers. "He can't stay in this world much longer. He needs to go back to the spirit world to regain his strength. What I did was just a...a Band-Aid." She drank from the mug again and grimaced at the increased alcohol content. "That thing was eating him. It was stealing his energy. Tiger's been my guardian as far back as I can remember. I'm not letting that happen to him again."

Zach reached for Deegie's hand and curled his fingers around hers. "First thing in the morning, Deeg. I promise."

She snatched her hand away and used it to delve into the chip bag. "Alright," she said. "Tiger will be okay until then, I suppose, but I'm going as soon as the sun comes up. With or without you."

* * *

Zach's Jeep was the only vehicle that would start the next morning, and the three of them, bundled in extra layers, made the intrepid journey over icy roads to Deegie's house on the other side of town. Midway up Fox Lane, the road was blocked by emergency vehicles and grim-faced policemen. Whirling red lights turned the fallen snow a lurid pink. A couple of paramedics had just finished loading a blanket-covered body into the back of an ambulance. They left the back doors yawning open, then stepped to the side of the road for a smoke. The covered body was in full view; apparently there was no need to rush.

Sitting in the back, Gilbert leaned forward and framed his face between the two front seats. "Wow!" he said with a weird enthusiasm. "I wonder what happened."

"Nothing good, from what I can see." Deegie swallowed her annoyance. Gilbert's voice was a little too cheerful for such a somber scene, and he'd hosed himself down with drugstore body spray this morning. The sickly scent filled the entire vehicle.

Zach, more sedate than his younger brother, simply said, "Oh geez."

A police officer strolled up to the idling Jeep, trailing white puffs of his breath behind him, and he made motions at Zach to roll down the window. Zach immediately complied.

"Hey, what's going on, officer? Any way we can get by?"

"That's my house up there," Deegie said, pointing helpfully.

Gilbert said nothing for once; he just sat there and reeked.

"Hikers coming down the mountain found a body in the woods a few hours ago. That's about all I can tell you. It'll probably be in this morning's paper. You can go on through; we're about done." He turned away without waiting for a reply, then moved his cruiser from the middle of the road and waved them through with an air of great importance.

"Well that's just great." Deegie spoke first as they pulled into the driveway. "I've got a pissed-off demon in my basement and a ghost hiding out on the second floor, and now somebody finds a dead guy in the woods behind my house. And to think I moved out here because I was craving the isolation." She cupped her hands and blew into them, then opened the door. "Come on, you guys. Might as well tear up the kitchen floor too, huh?" She headed for the house, blazing a trail through the ankle-deep snow.

Zach and Gilbert followed her across the snow-covered yard, and Gilbert could not resist a glance over his shoulder at the gruesome tableau down the street. "She still wants to live here, can you believe that?" He tucked his hands under his arms and grinned with teeth that were beginning to rattle.

"I know. Damned if I would, though. She's pretty tough," said Zach.

"Well, this is *my* house, after all," Deegie said without turning around. "And yes, I heard you."

While the Altman brothers exchanged guilty glances, Deegie produced her house key and unlocked the front door. "I really don't know what we're going to see," she said as they stepped over the threshold. "Even though this thing is on lockdown, it can still mess with your head, believe me. Let's just say it will be quite a while before I eat chicken again."

The demon's mind-shattering cries began the second they entered the hallway, and the thrift-shop portraits leaned away from the walls and rolled painted cerulean eyes in their direction. The renderings of the young man and his bride strained and lunged against their moorings, the frames jittering madly against the wall in their desperation to get at the intruders.

"See what I mean?" Deegie shuddered and doubled her pace.

"We should cloak ourselves," Gilbert said, walking briskly to catch up with her. "And I think we need to familiarize ourselves with the various metaphysical, ah, issues we may encounter."

"You can cloak if you want to," Deegie said, and she observed with little surprise that Gilbert immediately produced a fountain of protective light, holding it over his head like an umbrella. "I can't afford to use the energy for it. There might be a real emergency later." She cocked a thumb over her shoulder at the gawking portraits. "That was just an illusion; creepy as hell, but it can't hurt you."

"Oh shit, that was intense!" Zach's voice was a hoarse whisper, and his widened eyes stared straight ahead. "Like when I used to party with that garage band."

"What?" Deegie paused, scowling.

"Nothing, nothing." Zach coughed into his gloved hands, then rubbed them together rapidly. "Show us where."

Tiger Spirit did not greet her as they approached the kitchen, but Deegie sensed his presence by the door to the basement and paused to stroke his head. "It's almost over," she soothed. "All will be well, I promise you."

She flipped on the light and stood in the middle of her spotlessly clean, eclectically decorated kitchen. The stove was the stove and the fridge was the fridge. There was no zombie chicken; there were no rabid fruits. She glanced around, checking for signs of life, then pointed at the floor next to the refrigerator.

"Here," she said.

The demon went silent, as though it were extremely interested in what they were doing. The sensation of being watched with unseen eyes intensified as Zach took careful aim with the claw end of his hammer and pried away layers of linoleum and decades of grime.

The three of them sat on the cold floor of Deegie's kitchen, staring in wonderment at the false floorboard that Zach's hammer had finally revealed. The air was laced with their frosty exhalations. Dust motes, decades old, glimmered and drifted in the shaft of winter sunshine pouring through the window.

"Well then, shall we have a look?" Gilbert said.

"Open it," Deegie said.

Zach poked a screwdriver through the hole in the board and levered upwards. The loose board came up easily, with a sound like ripping canvas. A burlap bag, wrinkled and coated with dust, lay in the shallow recess. He gave the bag a gentle prod with the screwdriver, then picked it up and set it on the floor. "Feels heavy," he noted.

"Maybe more than one book?" Gilbert's eyes gleamed with avarice as he reached for the bag, but his brother caught him by the sleeve.

"Let Deegie open it," Zach said, and he slid the bag closer to her.

The drawstring broke when she tugged on it; the decades-old cord gave way with a soft *pop,* and Deegie paused to rub her fingers on her jeans. Her hand hesitated at the mouth of the bag, then plunged inside to grasp the contents. The burlap, fragile with age, split open to reveal two small leather-bound books and a sprinkling of dried mouse turds. "Two. You were right, Gilbert." She rubbed her fingers together and picked up the first book.

The binding cracked when she opened the book, and a shower of yellowed newspaper clippings fell into her lap. Gilbert snatched one up before the others could protest, and he managed to unfold it without tearing it. "Missing person," he said after reading it. "Elisabeth Lanyon, age 70. Presumed lost in a snowstorm." He picked up another clipping. "Another one about the same lady. Presumed dead this time."

"Elisabeth," Deegie's voice broke a little. "It's Lisbet. She wasn't lost in a snowstorm, she was murdered by the same jackasses who put these books in the floor." She scanned a few pages of the dusty book in her lap. "It's a journal, I think. I don't see any spells, just entries, like a diary." She picked up the other book and winced as if she'd been bitten. The leather binding was colder than the deepest grave. It fell from her hands and the three of them saw that the book was coated in a rime of frost—save for the melted spots left by Deegie's fingers.

"Holy shit, that's *gotta* be it!" Zach poked at the fallen book and recoiled when he too felt the unearthly chill. "Is this safe? I mean, you guys know what you're doing, right?"

"I don't know," Deegie admitted. "I've never dealt with anything like this before." She blew on her hands to warm them, and turned to Gilbert. "How about you, Gilbert? Any experience with demons?"

He shook his head, still eyeing the Book of Shadows lying on the floor. "No. Can't say that I have, but I do know of a paranormal group in Oregon who might be able to assist us."

"No." Deegie said with a firm shake of her head. "If word gets out about this house, I'll never have a moment's peace. The last thing I want is a bunch of people tramping around, scaring Lisbet, or doing a slow drive-by while they rubberneck my home. I'll do all the research I need to do, I'll experiment with different techniques if I have to, and if you're scared, you don't even have to help me. It's a long shot, but maybe that Murphy guy can tell us a little more about what he knows. But I don't want anyone else to know about this. Understand?"

Gilbert stared at her incredulously, but did not object. "Okay, Deegie," he said. "And I'll still help you. We might have to pay off Shit Storm in booze, though." He got to his feet and took a long cylindrical box from his coat pocket. "I'd like to have a look at your Locking Spell, if you don't mind. Just to make sure that thing isn't going to get out anytime soon." He opened the box as he spoke, revealing two lengths of rounded, tapered wood on a pillow of blue velvet. "I'm better prepared this time, fortunately." Gilbert took the two pieces of wood and screwed them together like a pool cue, then held up the object, making sure that Deegie and Zach saw what it was: a custom-designed wand, fitted with moonstones and engraved with his initials on the end.

Deegie's derisive snort slipped out before she could stop it. "You use a wand?"

"Most of the time, yes." Gilbert buffed one of the moonstones with the edge of his T-shirt. "Don't you?"

"Uh, no. Not since I was a little kid, but, um...let's go check out the door."

Gilbert walked out of the room with his lovely wand held out in front of him like an offering, and Deegie waited until he was out of earshot before leaning close to Zach and whispering, "A wand? And you call *me* a walking cliché?"

Zach grinned as he slid the books into a plastic shopping bag. "Yup. He has a whole collection of them. He has a crystal ball, too." He tucked the bag, with its grim contents, into the inside pocket of his coat. "See what I've had to live with all my life? Gil's not a bad guy, he's just..." He cleared his throat and pointed in the direction of the basement. "Let's go check out your Locking Spell and get the hell out of here."

As Deegie and Zach approached the basement door, they noticed Gilbert standing far to the side of it, clutching his wand and looking distressed. "Your, ah, guardian is a little upset with me," he said. "Such a touchy tiger." Gilbert rubbed his backside ruefully, and Deegie didn't need to ask what had happened.

"I'm not surprised," she said as she knelt to embrace her long-suffering guardian. "Tiger's going to die if we don't get rid of this demon. He's weak. He's been in the physical world for too long, protecting me."

Tiger grunted and swiped his rough tongue across Deegie's cheek.

Zach peered hard at the empty space in front of Deegie. "Deeg? Is he...is Tiger something that only witches can see? Because I don't see anything. I can hear and smell him, but there's absolutely nothing in front of you."

"I don't see him either, Zach. Tiger is a spirit animal; he doesn't have a physical body. But he's my friend, and I don't want to lose him. Let's go. We have a lot of work to do."

"One sec," said Gilbert. He tapped his fancy wand over Deegie's Locking Spell and cleared his throat importantly. "Just making sure this door is secure for now."

The door had been fused in place by Deegie's white-hot energy. Nothing short of a fireman's axe could take it down, but Gilbert's need to have the final say prevailed.

"You did a damn fine job with this, I gotta say," he said as he unscrewed the pieces of his wand and tucked it back into its carrying case. "Looks like your little *handicap* hasn't slowed you down at all."

***

The photo on front page of the newspaper was partially obscured by the yellow plastic strip, but Deegie recognized the man's lumpy nose, square jaw, and vacant stare immediately. She brought the bundle of newspapers inside the shop and set them on the counter next to the register. The teakettle whistled behind her. Tea and instant oatmeal first, a little deep breathing, and then she would read the headline, although she already had a pretty good idea of what it was going to say. After that, she planned on reading as much of the journal as she could. She moved the space heater closer to her stool, snipped the yellow binding on the newspapers, and ate her hasty breakfast while she read the front page:

Body Found in Woods Identified

"Jarvis Murphy, a local man well-known in the downtown area, was found dead Tuesday morning in the heavily wooded area behind Fox Lane. The cause of death has not been determined, but foul play is not suspected. The deceased was discovered by hikers who were returning to town before the storm..."

She put the paper down without finishing the story. She didn't know the old fart, and he had been a huge pain in the ass, but she couldn't help but feel a pang of sadness. And how perfectly odd that the one who had warned her about the house in the first place had died only a few hundred yards behind it. Deegie put the newspapers in the rack without looking at the headlines again and unlocked the door for her first customers of the day.

Once the morning rush had ebbed, Deegie sat behind the counter at The Silent Cat, warm, comfortable, and fortified with cup after cup of herbal tea. Bast drowsed on her lap, and the fragile journal from the house lay open in front of her. She'd tucked the Book of Shadows, still wrapped in its plastic bag, into a drawer under the register. As much as she hated to admit it, she wanted another witch present when *that* particular book was opened and examined, and she wished she hadn't brought it with her. She felt its malign presence every time she went to the register to ring up a customer's purchase. She couldn't wait until this was all over and she could throw the accursed thing into the fireplace.

The journal was just an ordinary little diary, crammed with line after line of hectic, disjointed scribblings, but Deegie couldn't stop reading it. In those delicate, yellow-edged pages, she was finding out more than she ever wanted to know about who was responsible for the jar of fingers.

October 2, 1927

We have found a room to rent, Edwin and I. Hallelujah! It isn't much, but we won't be sleeping on the streets anymore. The landlady is odd, but she doesn't charge much, thank God. We desperately need money.

October 5, 1927

Edwin again. Those books of his! He claims that the answer to our predicament is an offering to a demon called Chul. He says we will be rewarded with riches beyond compare if we do so. I am skeptical, but hungry.

October 15, 1927

I'm afraid he's really going to do it this time. Everything is ready. If this spell works, we will have everything our hearts have ever desired, but what if it doesn't? "Oh, Johnathan," he tells me, "you do nothing but worry."

October 30, 1927

Edwin has prepared the basement and all the equipment. Tomorrow night begins our new life as rich men. Ha! And Father said we would never amount to much! All hail the demon Chul, bringer of money and fame!

November 1, 1927

It is done. Edwin has summoned the great Chul. I have underestimated my brother's abilities. All that was required was a small sacrifice. The old crone will never miss them. Ha! Too many damn cats anyway!

Deegie slammed the book closed and shoved it away, unable to read anymore. They killed Lisbet and her cats to appease the demon! "Oh those bastards..." She picked up a sleepy Bast and nuzzled his fuzzy head. Any fear that she may have felt regarding her unusual situation vanished and was replaced with a seething rage. Not even when she'd caught Spencer cheating had she been so angry. "I will take care of everything, Lisbet," she whispered. "I promise you this."

She remembered the demon Chul from the stories her father used to tell her when her mother wasn't around. While he wasn't the most fearsome of all the demons, Chul was far from harmless. She remembered her father's description of Chul: a chubby red baby with horns and a pitchfork. As she grew older, she realized he'd turned the demon into a cartoon so his tales wouldn't frighten her as much. Now she knew why. The thing in the basement was a smoky, tentacle-waving horror.

After a brief rush of customer activity, Deegie went to the herbs shelf and selected jars of Asafetida, Mullein, and Scotch Broom, herbs especially useful for making protective powders. The special blend had served her well for years, in all manner of negative circumstances, but she had never dealt with anything like Chul before. The potent protective powder could easily be rendered as effective as a BB gun on a grizzly bear. Willing to take the chance, she ground the herbs into a fine powder with a mortar and pestle while she put together a plan of attack, which Gilbert would no doubt try to revise to his way of thinking. As she worked, she eyed the drawer where she'd stashed the Book of Shadows and felt the baleful energy that seeped through. It seemed to be mocking her from its hiding place, challenging her to open it and discover its dark secrets. For the first time since she was a child, Deegie found herself wishing her father were still in this realm; if anyone knew what to do, it would be him.

CHAPTER ELEVEN

WHEN DEEGIE RETURNED TO THE brothers' house later that evening, she was relieved to see that Gilbert had not come home yet. She would need his help, certainly, and soon, but she relished the chance to speak, uninterrupted, to Zach about what she had read so far in the journal. He met her at the door, and the smile died on his lips when he saw the look on her face.

"Guess you heard about old Shit Storm, huh?" He took her coat for her and hung it in the foyer closet.

"Yeah, I saw it in the paper this morning. Poor old drunk. I kind of feel bad about the wisecrack I made yesterday. This is even worse, though." She held up the shopping bag with the two old books inside. "I took these to work with me and did a little reading. I found out who the 'bad men' were, and—oh, Zach, it's just awful! You're not going to believe this!"

"Hey, hey, easy now." Zach put an arm around her and led her to the couch. "Let's get you warmed up and settled in, and you can tell me all about it."

She declined his offer of warmed-over chicken nuggets, and with Bast wrapped safely in her arms, she told him what she had read about Lisbet's cats. "It gets even worse, I'm sure," she said, trailing a fingertip over the newspaper clippings that had been tucked inside the journal. "Those men killed Lisbet, Zach. I know they did. I just couldn't bring myself to read about it."

He picked up the journal almost reverently, flipped through the pages, and began to read while Deegie sat quietly and stared at the Book of Shadows, still wrapped in plastic and sitting on the coffee table. After a few minutes of reading, Zach cleared his throat repeatedly; his Adam's apple bobbing up and down under his red beard. He closed the book with his finger marking his place and said, "Well, then."

"Something?" She knew he had just read a particularly distressing entry, but she waited for him to explain anyway.

"Uh, well...yeah. I'm sorry Deeg." He opened the journal and handed it to her. "Here," he said. "Just read."

Deegie lowered her eyes to the cramped, black-ink handwriting, and steeled herself for what she was about to learn.

November 5, 1927

Something has gone wrong, but Edwin refuses to admit it. What good is wealth when you cannot enjoy it? It screams down there, all night, and during the day, the raised demon Chul breathes down my neck and whispers the most awful things in my ear. Black, stinking, hellish thing! No amount of money is worth this. Edwin will not send it back, but he must or I fear we will both go mad. The old woman is oblivious to the situation. She does not even realize what we have done. Bless her ignorant soul, for she is most fortunate.

November 7, 1927

Edwin understands now. The thing screamed in his room all night long. It must be sent back to the depths of hell! We must reverse the spell before it is too late. Chul is full of false promises. I should have known. I should never have strayed from the church. Edwin says we need a sacrifice again, and I'm sure he doesn't mean a couple of mangy cats. God help us.

November 10, 1927

It is done, but Edwin did a messy job. I cleaned all afternoon. How were we to know that it would kill her? We hadn't planned on that. We just needed a little blood, a bit of flesh. She has no family, he says. No one will know. God knows, though. He knows what we did. That glass must never break. God help the person who breaks that glass.

"So they did kill her. She wasn't lost in a snowstorm! Those idiots killed her, just like she said!" Deegie closed the book with a slap and tossed it onto the coffee table. She had no desire to read the rest of it. "They buried her in the backyard, where she'd started a little cemetery for her cats. If we dug there, we would find her."

"Do you think we should?"

"No. I offered, and she got very upset. She wants to be with her cats. Besides, what good would it do? Everyone involved is long dead. There's no one left to punish. I want her to stay where she is, and I'll plant new rosebushes over the spot." She swallowed hard against the lump rising in her throat; hot tears of sadness and rage coursed down her cheeks. "Those were her fingers in that jar, weren't they?"

"Yeah. Edwin and his brother, Johnathan, set a trap. They did a spell with a jar or something. He explains it more in his next entry. They used her fingers as bait. I don't think they meant to kill her, but I guess, well, she was old, and the shock…Anyway, that thing's been trapped in that jar since 1927."

Deegie made a fist with the hand that wasn't holding Bast. "Assholes," she said. Although the men who'd killed Lisbet were, in all probability, dust in their graves by now, she wished she could somehow resurrect them and bring them to justice herself, preferably piece by piece.

Gilbert burst noisily through the front door, stomping snow off his boots and shaking more out of his hair. Under his arm was a brown paper bag folded around something that looked suspiciously like a liquor bottle. He tossed it to Zach, saying, "I thought we could use a little liquid courage before we go demon-busting. Hello, Deegie. Nice to see you this evening."

She returned his greeting, hoping he wouldn't notice her tears and fake smile. How Zach managed to put up with his arrogant, condescending brother was beyond her. "We've discovered some pretty tragic stuff in the journal," she said, and she moved to the far end of the couch so he could sit down. "Lisbet was murdered by those men and used as bait to trap the demon. Those were her fingers in the jar. They killed her cats, too."

"Sounds like some sort of trapping spell with a human flesh and blood sacrifice," Gilbert said, and he sat between Deegie and Zach, bringing a dwindling pocket of cold outdoor air with him. "You have to bring out the good stuff if you want to trap them. Human blood is a delicacy to demons; they can't resist it. But we don't want to just trap this guy, do we?"

Deegie cringed and stared at the floor.

"Yeah, something like that." Zach scowled at the journal sitting on the coffee table. "That's messed up, man. Poor old lady. I think they just wanted her fingers and some blood, but..." he left the sentence unfinished, and Deegie could tell he was trying not to upset her any more than she already was.

"Well, we won't need to do anything like that, I'm sure."

"No. We won't." Deegie's words came out much harsher than she had intended, but she made no apology. She nudged the Book of Shadows closer to Gilbert, using the side of her hand and wishing she didn't have to touch it at all. "Here. Open this and look at it. Find their spell for raising demons, and we'll start from there."

"Alright then." Gilbert sniffed loudly and stripped the plastic bag from the antique tome. "Gah, it's *cold!*"

"It's evil," Deegie said.

While Gilbert pored over the Book of Shadows, Zach went to the kitchen and returned with three plastic cups. He lined them up on the table and poured into each a generous shot of the whiskey that Gilbert had brought. Deegie downed hers immediately, hoping it would take the edge off the fierce anger she still felt. The liquor burned all the way down, and she tried not to gag.

"I made protection powder today, by the way." she said. "A lot of it." She produced the jar of powdered herbs from her purse and set it next to the bottle of whiskey. "We're going to need it."

Gilbert glanced up from the book in his lap. "Did you use asafetida and bay leaf?" He tapped the side of the jar of powdered herbs and shook his head. "This doesn't look right to me."

A JAR OF FINGERS

Deegie really wanted to stick the jar of powder in Gilbert's mouth to keep him from talking any more, but she drew a deep breath and willed herself to endure Zach's brother with grace and style. "Asafetida, mullein, and Scotch broom. There is more than one recipe for protection powder, you know. Read the book, please."

Gilbert squinted at the jar of powder again, wisely keeping his mouth shut, and returned to the Book of Shadows. Zach and Deegie remained silent while he read, and Bast frolicked on the carpet with the cap from a beer bottle. Outside, the snow started falling again, in hard, hail-like pebbles that ticked against the windowpanes. Although she was safe now, in her head Deegie still heard the horrifying shrieks and wails of the demon Chul.

After ten minutes of reading, Gilbert closed the Book of Shadows and cleared his throat importantly. "I think I've got it," he said. "I'm surprised these two inexperienced Normal Ones were able to raise an actual demon by using such a crude spell. Definitely not a professional spell, not something I would use anyway." He sniffed in distain. "But somehow they were able to do it. It's a good thing this isn't a sophisticated spell, actually. I think all we need to do is a simple reversal."

"A reversal? What's that, like just saying the spell backwards or something?" Zach gulped down his whiskey then poured another shot into his empty plastic cup.

"Pretty much," said Gilbert. "With a few minor adjustments, we should be able to send it back to the Underworld with no trouble." He winked at Deegie and added, "I'm kinda surprised you haven't tried that already, Deeg."

With that statement, Deegie reached her limit, and her voice rose along with her ire. "Are you joking? You saw that damn thing! Do you really think I would abandon all common sense and take it on all by myself without even knowing what I was dealing with? And with my handicap? Are you crazy?"

He infuriated her even further by laughing at her outrage. "Lesser demons will sometimes puff themselves up, you know, to make themselves look more intimidating." He snorted and picked up his cup. "Besides, what are the chances that a couple of Normal Ones could raise a full demon?"

"Damn it, Gilbert!" Deegie stood up abruptly, her pale blue eyes alight with anger. "This is *not* a lesser demon! They raised Chul! You know who he is, don't you? You should, since you know everything! They sacrificed a harmless old woman and some of her pets to do it! This isn't just some mischievous imp!" She slapped her hands together for emphasis and sat down again, her cheeks blazing with color and her lips trembling.

"Uh, Deeg?" Zach said, as gently as he could. "To be fair, Gil didn't know that. He didn't read the journal, remember?"

She nodded and buried her face in her hands. "I know. I'm sorry, Gilbert, it's just—you don't know everything, okay? You don't."

"Been trying to tell him that his entire life," Zach muttered.

"Okay," Gilbert relented. "I can be kind of an ass, I know. I'm the one who should be apologizing. Sorry, Deeg. And no, I've never heard of Chul." Embarrassed, he lowered his head and fiddled with the cap to the whiskey bottle.

"I'll be damned," said Zach. "I think this is the first time I've *ever* heard ol' Gil apologize for *anything*!"

Gilbert's blush deepened, and he nodded and shrugged. "She's right, I admit it. I *don't* know everything. I've just never had a pretty girl call me out on it before." He offered Deegie his hand. "Truce?"

Truce? She wanted to smack him. She wished they were back in her own house so she could have the satisfaction of ordering him out. Yet despite Gilbert's infuriating, condescending manner, she knew she needed him; she couldn't do this on her own. Not that she would ever tell *him* that.

"Of course, Gilbert," she said hastily. "Let's just forget it." She gave his hand a brief shake, then tapped her nails against the jar of Protection Powder. "Can we get back to this now?"

"Why don't you tell us what *you* think we should do, Deegie?" Gilbert leaned forward attentively, and his humbled smile was sincere this time. "I really do want to know, I promise."

"Alright then." She resettled herself on the couch cushions and folded her hands on her knees. "First I'll tell you what I think we *shouldn't* do: the spell reversal. They summoned Chul with a blood sacrifice, then they shut him down the same way. If we try to reverse the spell to banish him for good, wouldn't we need to start the same way? With a blood sacrifice of some sort?"

Gilbert tented his fingers under his chin as he pondered this. "That could be," he said. "I never considered that."

"Well, I refuse to sacrifice anything to any demon for any reason. It's murder. Besides, my mother taught me better than that. My father...well...that's a story for another time."

"What do you suggest, then? Tell me."

Deegie's solution was more ethical, but potentially deadly. "We open a hell portal," she said, "and we shove the sucker back through."

The Altman brothers gaped in silent astonishment, and Deegie, not at all surprised by their reaction, leaned back in her seat and waited for them to process her suggestion.

"Is that, ah, is that safe?" Zach finally asked.

"No, not at all," Deegie replied calmly. "But neither is living in a house with a demon trapped in the basement."

Gilbert coughed nervously into his fist. "Do you know how to do this, Deegie? Because if you do, then I have most definitely underestimated you."

"I've never actually done it before, but yes, I know the basics. My dad had an entire shelf of books dedicated to the dark arts. I read every one of them. Even took notes."

"You mean your father was a..."

"A dark witch, yes." Deegie finished Zach's sentence for him, then changed the subject. She would tell them another time, perhaps when this nightmare was over. "We will need black candles, of course. I have an entire box of them at the shop. And red paint. And, naturally, we'll need some live bait. The Gatekeepers of the Underworld aren't going to open the door for nothing, you know."

"Live bait?" Zach chuckled nervously. "Damn, that's pretty hardcore. What are you going to use for that?"

"You," Deegie said.

CHAPTER TWELVE

"TELL ME AGAIN HOW THIS is going to work," Zach said for the third time as he stood in the kitchen doorway and watched Deegie and Gilbert at work. The two witches had painted a gigantic inverted pentagram on the floor and surrounded it with strategically placed black candles.

"You stand in the middle of the pentagram," Deegie replied once more. "Then Gil and I will close the circle and put a ring of protection around you with light, salt, and the powder I made. We will chant the words that summon the Gate Keepers. When they see their offering and they approve, they will open the portal to accept you. Now here's where it gets tricky. At the same time the portal opens, Gilbert will unseal the basement door and let Chul out. Chul will see you in the pentagram and believe me, he's going to charge at you. All you need to do is jump out of the way before he reaches you so Gilbert and I can blast him from behind and knock him into the portal. If we can close it before he realizes he's been tricked, then this will all be over."

"Holy shit," Zach whispered. "What if something goes wrong? Then what do I do?"

"Don't worry about that. As long as you stay right in the middle of the pentagram and don't move until we say so, you'll be fine. And when we tell you to run, you do it. Understood?"

Zach wiped his palms down the legs of his jeans, his face distressed. "Yeah," he said. "Gotcha."

Deegie struggled to smile and didn't make it. After glancing at Gilbert, who was intent on getting the lines of the pentagram just right, she led Zach over by the staircase so she could talk to him in private. "Hey, you don't have to do this, you know," she told him. "You can back out and I won't hold it against you, I promise. This is some is some pretty intense stuff, even for witches. I can think of something else."

Zach shook his head firmly despite his nervousness. "No. I won't back out. I trust you, Deeg."

"Thank you, Zach. I won't let you get hurt. Promise."

"I'm gonna hold you to that," he said.

"Zach? You okay?"

He reddened and rubbed the back of his neck. "Yeah, yeah, I'm good, I just...am I supposed to kiss you right now or something? That's what usually happens in the movies, anyway. I really suck at this."

Deegie pressed her lips together and regarded him before replying. "Not now," she said. "But maybe after all this is over, we can discuss it over nachos."

"I'm gonna hold you to that too, Deeg."

Tiger Spirit, still at his post by the basement door, interrupted them with a growl and a huff as he paced back and forth across the hallway. The rasp of his thick footpads and the ticking of his claws against the floor provided counterpoint to the cacophony of howls and shrieks from the other side of the door. Both entities, demon and guardian spirit, could sense the restless energy of the humans. Another entity was aware too. From the top of the staircase, Lisbet's clear, achingly beautiful voice drifted down to them as she sang the words to her favorite song.

Zach paused, his head cocked to one side. "I hear...is that...?"

"Lakmé's Flower Duet," Deegie told him. "Lisbet loves to sing."

Zach went to the foot of the staircase and peered up into the shadows. "Hello? Can you talk to me, Lisbet?"

Lisbet went silent at the sound of Zach's voice, stopping mid-note, like someone had pulled the plug of an antique radio from a wall socket.

"She won't come down," Deegie said. "She's afraid of men."

"I can certainly understand why. Poor old gal."

Deegie looked away from him and took in the macabre sight on the floor in front of the basement door: the blood-red pentagram, the uneasy flames of the somber black pillar candles, and the ring of Protection Powder surrounding it all. Zach would be standing in the middle of all this very shortly, but she would not allow her thoughts to project any further than that. Despite the horrendous noise from the creature in the basement she felt entirely confident that the nasty, bellowing thing would be gone for good shortly.

"Are you ready, Zach?" Gilbert's voice was just above a whisper and tinged with a mixture of awe and trepidation. He had left an open spot in the ring of protection powder, and one candle remained unlit. "Enter the circle here. Then I will close it behind you."

Before entering the magic circle, Zach paused in front of Deegie and gently took her by the shoulders. "Hey, listen Deeg. Just in case something happens, I—"

"Nothing's going to happen to you, Zach. I promise you that. Just stay in the circle until I tell you to run. Gilbert I are going to kick this thing's ass. You'll see." The light from the candles cast an amber glow over Deegie's pale cheeks and reflected in her black hair. Although her expression was grim, a light of fierce confidence shone on her face.

Zach surprised her by reaching out and cupping her face in his hands. "What I was *going* to say, is I think you're pretty damn cool for a walking cliché." He brushed the curls off her forehead and pressed a kiss there. "Let's get this show on the road." He turned away before she could reply and stepped into the circle.

"You'll be okay, bud. I promise," Gilbert reassured his brother as he closed the circle with a final sprinkle of protection powder. He lit the last candle and Zach was enclosed in the pentagram.

Deegie approached the circle and she and Gilbert exchanged a glance. She grasped his hand and held it tightly. "Don't let go of me," she said. "In order to make this work, I'll need to draw energy from you; I can't do this by myself. When the portal opens, I want you to blast open that basement door. When Chul comes out, I'm going to give it everything I've got and blow him right through that portal. I should have enough energy left to close it afterwards. Got it?"

"*Should?* What do you mean, you *should* have enough? What happens if you don't?"

"Then you'll have to do it, of course, and quickly. If Chul figures out he's being tricked, we're all dead."

The pitch of Gilbert's voice rose a notch. Beads of sweat appeared on his forehead and gleamed in the candle light. "Deegie, I've never closed a hell portal before. Crap, I've never even opened one!"

"Well you're in good company then, because I haven't either."

Tiger huffed behind them, and Gilbert felt his warm breath against his back. "What about your guardian? Can he help?"

Deegie shook her head. "Tiger does not have magical powers," she said. "He is a protective spirit." She reached for Tiger's head without looking down, and the great beast rumbled his reassurance. "Tiger's so weak now, Gilbert. He can't hold on much longer, but he will not return to the Spirit World until this is over."

"But what do I *do*, Deegie? If you fall, and it's all left up to me—"

"Hush! Just listen! If I fall I can still be your conduit. Grab my hand. I'll say the words, and you send the energy. But, no matter what happens, don't show this bastard any fear. These things feed off of fear. Believe me, if Chul knows you're afraid, it will only make him stronger."

"Oh, holy crap..." Gilbert let out a long, ragged breath and struggled to maintain his composure. "Look, I underestimated you, big time. I had no idea you were so...so knowledgeable. I thought you were just a...you know."

"A what? A second-rate witch?" Deegie smirked.

"Uh, something like that, yeah." Gilbert blushed furiously and turned his head away.

A tremendous blow from beneath their feet nearly knocked them over, and from the spaces between the floorboards, a few foul black tentacles of smoke rose up and swayed back and forth as if testing the air. Gilbert raised his hand without thinking, and a white-hot bolt of concentrated energy shot forth and obliterated the escapees. Chul's incessant roars of protest grew louder and more insistent.

"Don't show it any fear?" Gilbert repeated Deegie's words. "Sure, Deeg. No pressure."

Still holding tightly to his hand, Deegie led Gilbert to the magic circle where Zach stood waiting. "Ready?"

Zach opened his mouth to speak, but only nodded instead. Gilbert and Deegie began to walk the perimeter of the circle, and Deegie intoned the ancient chant that would open a gate to the very depths of hell. More of the smoggy tentacles broke free from their confines and groped blindly for anything they could grab. Chul screamed in rage and a barrage of blows nearly knocked the basement door off its hinges. Crumbles of Deegie's Locking Spell came loose and fell in dying spirals to the floor. Tiger's furious bellow shook the air. The demon was breaking free.

When the circle was complete and blazing with light, Deegie called out to the ancient ones who guarded the gates to hell: "Keepers of the Unholy Gates! We bring to you a sacrifice and we beseech you to assist us!" Her voice rose in a hoarse shout as she strained to be heard above the infernal racket of Chul and the weakening roars of Tiger Spirit. She repeated her request, louder still, and she felt Gilbert's energy flow from his hand and into her body. She thrummed with power from the very core of her being, a sensation she'd never felt before. Every hair on her body stood on end and a rash of goose bumps rose on her skin. "Open the gates and take our offering of blood and flesh! Open the gates, we beseech you!"

The air in front of the magic circle wavered then, as a heat mirage wavers in the distance on a desert road, and a sound like distant thunder reverberated through the house: it was working. Deegie called out to the Gate Keepers a third time, and a ragged slit formed in the center of the disrupted air with a sound like a gigantic pair of hands clapping. The slit yawned wider and the cacophonous shrieks of the damned poured forth in an unholy flood. Gouts of flame and black smoke shot out in a boiling, choking miasma. Deegie saw Zach's legs buckle and he dropped to his knees in the center of the pentagram with his arms wrapped around his head and his eyes screwed tightly shut. *Don't move, Zach!* She willed him to receive her frantic thought form. *I know you're scared, but* please *don't move yet!*

The rip between the realms widened, its edges smoldering, and from behind the wall of flame came a voice that reeked of evil and bad intent. *"MORTAL WOMAN, WHAT DO YOU SEEK?"*

Deegie had prepared for everything but this; she hadn't considered that the Gate Keeper of the Underworld would actually speak to her. Thinking quickly, she bowed her head and replied. "We seek guidance from the Great Ones! We desire to learn of your dark ways and join your hellish forces!" Internally, she fluttered on the near edge of panic. What if her ruse wasn't convincing enough? If not, there was every chance that she had just condemned all three of them to an unspeakable fate. Huddled in the center of the pentagram, Zach took his hands away from his face and stared hard at Deegie with hurt and frightened eyes. Gilbert drew in a shocked breath and tightened his hand around hers, but said nothing.

Oh please, guys, please! Just trust me on this, okay? Just play along, please just play along! The frantic thought resounded through her brain, and her heart flung itself against her ribs as if it were a trapped bird.

The voice from the portal was silent, as if pondering her request. Then, after a booming laugh that shook the old house to its very foundation, it said, *"THEN GIVE ME WHAT IS MINE!"*

From behind the undulating mass of flame, something approached the portal. Between shifting leaves of fire, Deegie saw the bulky silhouette of something hunched, black, and massive. A skeletal hand, ten times the size of a normal human's, burst through the curtain of hellfire and snatched avariciously at the red-bearded man in the center of the inverted pentagram.

"Zach! Now! Run!" Deegie screamed her warning just as Gilbert let go of her hand and raced for the basement door. Zach leaped for the edge of the circle and the hand slammed into the floor where he'd been just moments before. The bony fingers, each as big around as a lamp post, clutched at the spot where their prize had been, knocking over the candles, and smearing the Protection Powder and painted pentagram into a red goo. From behind her, she heard Gilbert's ragged cry of *"Patefacere ianua!"* and a shower of bright white sparks erupted from the door to the basement as he blasted away the last of her Locking Spell. With a resounding crack, the basement door exploded outwards in a hail of splinters and, bearing the fulsome reek of evil and decay, Chul was free.

Robed in ebony shadows, the escaped demon bellowed in triumph while its grape-like cluster of orange eyes rolled and squinted in the dazzling light of the open hell portal. Near the top of the nine-foot-tall mass of living blackness, a crescent mouth opened, revealing jagged, broken fangs that dripped with a viscous green fluid. Dazzled by the flames after its week of dark captivity, Chul was unable to see the two scurrying humans that slipped behind his back on either side, nor was he prepared for the tremendous blow that slammed into him from behind as Deegie unleashed her first bolt of energy. Chul was driven forward, closer to the fiery portal, and a large chunk of his shadow body was sheared away. Before the hellish beast could recover, Gilbert streamed furious bolts of energy from both hands, knocking the demon forward even further.

"Hit it again!" Deegie yelled over the combined racket of Chul and the snap and crackle of the flaming portal. "Again, Gilbert!"

She squeezed her eyes shut and took in great, shuddery breaths of the smoky, scalding air. The ghastly stink of Chul nearly made her retch, and her knees were already weak and rubbery from the huge amount of energy she'd just expended. An enormous, sizzling *whoosh* made her clap her hands over her ears: Gilbert had just unleashed another bolt. Her skin tingled as it passed overhead with just inches to spare. Tiny sparks, no bigger than pin heads, fell stinging onto her arms and shoulders.

"Damn it! You almost hit me, Gilbert!"

"Sorry!"

He stepped nimbly to her other side, and she heard the crackling *whoosh* again as Gilbert drove Chul forward once more. She opened her eyes to the sight of the black demon stumbling on rudimentary legs across the scorched and littered floor, urged forward against his will by the powerful male witch. The massive skeletal hand, still protruding from the portal, snatched and grabbed at Chul's dark, fog-like form, and the fleshless finger bones rattled and knocked together with a sound like gigantic castanets. The Gate Keeper of the Underworld realized he'd been fooled, and his outraged screams mixed with the roaring, guttural cries of Chul, also a victim of the clever humans' trickery.

Gilbert slammed another searing blast of white light into Chul, and he gave a whoop of victory when the demon staggered and slid halfway into the portal. "Deeg! It's working! We're sending the bastard back where he belongs!" He reached out for her arm without taking his eyes off the fiery scene before him, and he pulled her closer. "Let's nail him again! Both of us! You can do it, Deegie! One more!"

One more burst of energy. Yes, she could do that. It was working! Their plan was really working! Deegie widened her stance, braced her legs, and shook the hair out of her eyes. Raising her wildly trembling hands, she prepared to expel the last of her strength and send Chul back to the bowels of the Earth.

CHAPTER THIRTEEN

WITH A SHRIEK THAT BLEW out the windows in the kitchen, Chul wrenched himself away from the open hell portal and glowered at the two humans who dared to manipulate him. His glistening cluster of dull orange eyes rotated on their stems. Deegie saw the flames of the Underworld reflected in them. Before either of the witches could react, a thick black tentacle, solid and not at all like smoke, uncoiled from the demon's body and wrapped itself around Gilbert's waist. Then, like the arm of a demonic octopus, it tightened, clenched, and began dragging him upward towards the maliciously grinning crescent mouth and its ring of jagged, gnashing fangs. The blind, questing hand of bones from the Underworld, as if sensing a comrade in the furious Chul, crept across the floor, feeling its way to where hot blood and living flesh writhed and screamed in terror.

Deegie's mouth went slack and, in utter shock, she watched as Gilbert was lifted off the floor and hoisted towards the demon's unholy slavering maw. She raised her hands, intending to hammer Chul with the last of her power reserves, but realized that the risk of hitting Gilbert was too great. She grabbed for his flailing legs instead, wrapped her hands around his ankles, and pulled for all she was worth while she screamed for Zach, hoping desperately that he heard her.

"MINE! GIVE ME WHAT IS MINE! HOW DARE YOU SUMMON ME WITHOUT PAYMENT?!" The Gate Keeper of the Underworld shook the walls of the old house with his furious

foghorn voice, and his massive hand pawed and swiped at the unfortunate, dangling Gilbert.

"Zach! Help me! It's killing Gilbert! Zach!" Deegie screamed out for her friend again as she desperately clung to Gilbert's ankles. Above her head, she saw his bulging, horrified eyes looking down at her, saw his lips were moving in a silent prayer.

He managed to get a hand free, and he fired off a blast that struck the creeping, clattering hand of the Underworld Gate Keeper. The end of its cadaverous middle finger disintegrated in a riot of bone dust and red sparks. An ear-splitting bellow from the other side of the portal followed, and it retreated to the fiery depths, dragging its ruined digit. The jagged bone carved a long gouge in the wooden floor. Another random bolt from Gilbert's wildly waving hand missed its intended target and exploded against the kitchen wall. Cabinet doors flew open, and their load of plates, cups, and glasses smashed into jagged shards on the floor. Distracted by the noise of Gilbert's attempts to free himself, and the running footfalls of Zach as he pounded down the hall, Chul's grip on his prey loosened, and with another mighty yank from Deegie, Gilbert fell to the floor just as his brother returned.

Zach skidded in a pool of Chul's putrid slobber, and he went to one knee just as Gilbert dropped to the floor in front of him. Gilbert's shirt had come untucked, and his abdomen bore a row of bloody welts, but he was alive. On his hands and knees, Zach closed the distance between himself and his brother. Looming above the both of them, with insanely grinning mouth and staring, insectile eyes, was the thing from the basement.

The towering demon uncoiled a tentacle and sent it undulating in Zach's direction. Chul's foul appendage twined around his waist in a deadly noose, and as he was lifted off the floor, he uttered a single word:

"Deegie?"

Deegie shot a flash of light, bluish-white like a flashbulb, through the air, where it vaporized the deadly coil around Zach's body. Draped in whirling black smoke, with her upper lip lifted in a sneer, she screamed, "Leave them alone you bastard! Get out of my house!"

A high-pitched whine began in Deegie's ears, and she wobbled on her feet as she struggled to remain standing. The last of her powers left her in a string of fading pops and fizzles. Weak sparks dropped sluggishly from her fingertips. Her lungs burned as she pulled in huge, ragged breaths of the polluted air, and she asked, *prayed*, *BESEECHED* all the gods, all the goddesses to give her just a little more, just enough to send Chul back to the stinking pit from which he came.

The demon's clustered eyes rolled her way, dangling obscenely on their stalks. The drooling, cavernous mouth twisted into a mocking, sardonic smile.

From the pit of her stomach, a rage unlike any she had ever known rose upward in a burning trail and settled in her wildly pounding heart. This disgusting creature, this wretched, inhuman *thing* had invaded her new home, disrupted her life, stunk up her kitchen, and was now trying to kill her friends. She was barely conscious of her hands tightening into hard, white fists, and, despite the heat pouring through the open portal, icy ribbons of sweat trailed down her back and trickled between her breasts. *"Get out of my house! Go to Hell!"* She barely recognized her own voice as she screamed her demand. Deegie lifted her hands, palms out, and her mind gave one last gigantic *PUSH*. Blinding red lightning bolts shot from her fingertips, and Chul's entire left side exploded into inky shreds.

The force of the blow knocked Deegie off her feet and hurled her backwards into the wall. Multicolored stars blazed across her vision, and she sank to the floor, galvanized by a headache so agonizing it was nearly exquisite. Through fluttering, half-closed lids, she watched as Chul advanced on her, shrieking in outrage, his remaining eyes rolling crazily. He sent out another thick tentacle, and it bounced and hunched across the floor towards her while he gnashed his filthy, crooked fangs. Green foam poured out of his mouth and splattered down on her legs.

I hope I hurt you, asshole! Deegie tried to say it out loud but she hadn't the strength. *I hope I taste as horrible as you look. I hope I make you puke!*

Through the smoke and chaos, she saw Zach and Gilbert huddled against the wall next to the kitchen, and she struggled to raise her head, fought to form words. The Altman brothers had offered to help her and now they were going to die because she thought she could take on a demon. And Bast—what was to become of him? She'd left him at the brothers' house, sleeping on one of Zach's old T-shirts. Would he miss her? Would a kind soul take him in?

Chul crouched next to her now, and she felt the ghastly touch of his tentacles on her skin. Dank, scalding breath, reminiscent of an open sewer, blew into her face. With a mighty effort, she lifted a hand and raised her middle finger. *I hope you choke on me!*

On the outer edge of her vision, she saw something huge and tawny and moving fast. When it streaked past her, she realized what it was: Tiger! She saw him, actually *saw* him in his true form. He was breathtaking and magnificent, more beautiful than any mortal tiger. When he reared up on his hind legs, the top of his massive head brushed the ceiling. A swipe of his enormous paw relieved Chul of the rest of his eyes, but the wildly thrashing tentacle meant for Deegie snaked around Tiger's neck and tightened. Another writhing appendage materialized from inside Chul's body and waved menacingly in the air, looking for an opening.

Deegie clawed at the floor and pushed with her legs, trying desperately to crawl out of the way of the two battling titans, but even the slightest motion intensified her agony. A fist ground itself into the back of her T-shirt, and she felt herself being dragged across the floor. Zach's voice was loud in her ear, asking her over and over if she was okay. She shook her pain-filled head and wrenched it around, focusing as best she could on the supernatural battle taking place in her home.

Despite the choking tentacle around his neck, Tiger seemed to be gaining the advantage over Chul. The six-inch scythe-like claws of his front feet slashed and tore at Chul's already mutilated body, and Tiger propelled Chul steadily backwards towards the open portal. Chul, blinded and steadily weakening, offered little resistance; his dark body slipped over the threshold. He sent out three more appendages, all flailing and whiplashing through the air as he scrabbled madly for purchase. Bellowing and shrieking, he teetered on the edge, then fell into the flaming portal.

And he took Tiger with him.

Deegie heard someone screaming, hoarse, loud, and long, and it took several long seconds before she realized it was herself. Zach had her in his arms, checking her for injuries, and saying her name over and over, and she heard Gilbert's hoarse yell:

"Deegie, close it! Close the portal before it gets out!"

His hand sought hers, squeezing tightly. "Deeg, please! Just be my conduit, just say the words and I'll send the energy. *Say* them, Deegie!"

Zach pulled her into a sitting position and patted her cheeks smartly. "Say the words, honey. Come on, it's almost over. Don't let it get out again!"

She raised her head and fixed her eyes on the seething furnace that had just swallowed the friend she'd known since childhood. With the last of her strength, she shouted the words that she'd learned from her father's dark Book of Shadows: *"Claudere porta a malus!"*

Deegie felt a sharp, crackling sensation where her hand joined with Gilbert's, and she squinted against the brilliant light that streamed from his free hand. *"We revoke our invitation! We command all who would do us harm to leave this place and never return!"* She gasped out the rest of the words and held onto consciousness long enough to see the edges of the portal draw inward, slowly at first, then faster and faster. Just before it closed entirely, Deegie caught a glimpse of a black, man-shaped silhouette wearing a round-brimmed hat. The edges of the portal pinched shut with a whispery crackle, and the rift between the worlds was no longer there.

CHAPTER FOURTEEN

HER RETURN TO CONSCIOUSNESS WAS gradual. There were sounds, muffled at first: a ticking clock, snow blowing against a windowpane, a cat's purr. Deegie sensed soft light behind her closed lids, and she opened her eyes to see something small, black, and furry. Bast lay in a warm, purring ball next to her cheek, fully absorbed in licking his front paws. She lifted a hand to stroke his fur, but the motion set off a thunderbolt of pain that lanced through her head. *Best not to move. Take long, slow breaths. It will pass.* She recited the words she'd always used to comfort herself when recovering from an attack of Witch's Cramp, but they were woefully ineffective. The biggest comfort she had ever known was gone. Tiger Spirit was dead.

Deegie closed her eyes again and allowed the tears to come, sliding down her cheeks and wetting the pillowcase beneath her head. She eased herself back into the soft blackness of sleep, lulled by little Bast's enthusiastic purr.

When she awoke again the sound of snow against glass had been replaced with the murmuring drone of a TV set at low volume. A deep, careful breath brought her the scents of bacon and coffee. She sank down again, drifting for a while in that gray, fuzzy space between sleep and wakefulness, until a light knock and the distinctive rattle of dishes brought her around. Zach stood at the end of the bed, awash in morning sunlight. He moved aside a lamp on the nightstand and set down a tray of assorted breakfast items.

"Hey," he said. "Nice to see you awake. I was starting to get a little worried."

Deegie tried out her voice again and was pleased when it worked this time. "Zach. What time is it?"

"It's a little after ten, I guess."

"What day, I mean. How long?"

"How long have you been out, you mean? Just since last night."

He handed her a cup of pale yellow, delicately scented liquid: chamomile tea. She took it gratefully and let the warm steam soothe her face before taking a sip.

Gilbert appeared in the doorway, looking sheepish and hesitant. "Hi Deeg. Welcome back to the land of the living." He bent over her, in a nimbus of coffee and mouthwash, and kissed her cheek. "Feeling better?"

"Kinda. The pain in my head's gone, anyway." She sipped more tea and stared into her cup, her eyes welling. "But...Tiger..."

"I know. I'm so sorry, Deeg." Zach sat on the edge of the bed and brushed her tousled hair out of her eyes. "He was protecting you. He saved your life, you know."

"Yes, he did. He saved all of us."

Zach and Gilbert exchanged nervous glances, obviously unsure of what to say.

"I need to go home now," Deegie said, and she swung her legs out of the bed and tried to stand. Dizziness rushed her from all sides and a high-pitched whine sounded in her ears. Her legs buckled and she sat again. "Damn," she said mildly.

"Hey, take it easy." Gilbert grasped her shoulders and eased her back onto the pillows. "You kinda blew out your circuitry last night. It's going to be a while before you're back to normal again." Gilbert had lost his former arrogant tone, and his voice was now tinged with wonder and awe. "I've never seen a witch send out red light before," he added. "That was the most amazing thing I've ever experienced."

"I barely remember any of it," Deegie whispered, picking up her teacup. "I remember thinking we were all going to die, and I remember Tiger. That's all."

"Gil and I will go back and clean up that mess for you, but I think you should stay here for a few more days. Just until you're strong again." Zach tucked the blankets around her legs and handed her a plate with a raisin Danish on it. "Here. Eat something, honey. We will take care of things. I promise."

Deegie toyed with the raisins. "I have to talk to Lisbet. I need to make sure she's okay."

"Deeg, sweetheart, Lisbet's dead; she's a ghost. She'll be fine, I'm sure."

"I promised I'd do something special for her. I can't break that promise."

"Oh, you stubborn little thing." Zach's voice carried a hint of a chuckle despite Deegie's somber mood. "Take care of *you* first. Then we'll take care of your ghost, okay?"

She opened her mouth to protest further, then relented. He was right; they both were. She could hardly stand up, let alone confer with the ghost of a years-dead lady. "Okay," she said.

Deegie stayed where she was for the rest of the day, resting, grieving, and snuggling with Bast. When she slept, she dreamed of Tiger Spirit.

As in almost all cases of bereavement, Deegie's grief lessened as the days passed, but she still thought of Tiger almost constantly. Adjusting to life without him was strange, but Bast helped considerably; his endearing antics warmed her heart more than ever.

Zach and Gilbert had kept their promise about cleaning up the scene of the supernatural battle that had taken place in her home, and when she finally returned to 14 Fox Lane, not a trace remained of that horrific night. Gilbert had even replaced the dishes that had fallen from the cupboards and broken during the conflict. The basement was cleared out, hosed down, and locked up. Despite it being rendered perfectly safe, Deegie would not even entertain a thought of going down there again for a very long time.

* * *

On the morning of Thanksgiving, before even the birds were awake, Deegie stood in her gleaming white kitchen staring uncertainly at the twenty-pound turkey sprawled in the kitchen sink. The sight reminded her of another time, not long ago at all, when a horribly reanimated chicken had flopped and squirmed in this very same sink.

That's in the past, she reminded herself. *It wasn't real, it's all over. Now get over yourself and start cooking. The guys will be here before long. What are you going to feed them, Cheetos?*

Shaking her head briskly to knock the disturbing memory aside, she returned her attention to the open cookbook on the counter. She re-read the instructions on how to roast a turkey while a small saucepan of butter melted on the stove. After basting all its cold, bumpy flesh with the melted butter and whispering a prayer to whatever culinary gods there might be, Deegie put the turkey in the oven and set the timer. Thanksgiving was another first for her, and she'd studied the recipes she had planned for days in advance so as not to make a single mistake.

While she washed the dishes she'd used, Deegie caught a blur of motion outside the kitchen window and she looked up from her sink full of suds to see a dark shape moving through the trees behind her house. Filtered by the thick branches of the pines, the shape was indistinct, but large and moving fast as it came down the hill.

"What the heck is that?" She said the words aloud, and her heartbeat went from a sedate lope to a full gallop. She'd had more than her fair share of dark, mysterious shapes lately.

It's a coyote, or a bear, or some other sort of woodland creature, she rationalized to herself. *There are acres and acres of forest up in those hills, and the forest is full of critters; everybody knows that. Whatever it is, it isn't a demon. Now* cook, *dammit!*

Following her own orders, she reached up and snapped the curtains closed.

The temperature in the kitchen took a sudden drop, and she knew that Lisbet had materialized behind her. She'd been more active since Deegie and the Altman brothers had rid the house of the loathsome Chul, and she had fully materialized for Deegie on several occasions. Lisbet didn't always speak when she appeared, and she always kept her poor mutilated hand well hidden, but Deegie derived a great deal of comfort from her visits. Still, no amount of coaxing could persuade Lisbet to set aside her fear of men and come downstairs when Zach and Gilbert visited.

"Hello, Lisbet," Deegie said, and she turned around with a smile. "How are you today, my friend?"

Lisbet only giggled, and when Deegie looked down, she immediately saw why: Bast had followed Lisbet into the kitchen and was leaping back and forth, right though the ghost's misty form. It was easily one of the most bizarre things Deegie had ever seen. Lisbet glanced around the kitchen that had once belonged to her, and her soft, dove-grey eyes seemed to sparkle with delight at what she saw.

"I'm cooking Thanksgiving dinner, Lisbet!" Deegie said, gesturing expansively at the supplies she'd set out. "Did you cook Thanksgiving dinner in here, too?"

"Ducks and geese," said Lisbet.

"You must have been a great cook."

"Burn...so much food!" Lisbet said, and, giggling softly, she drifted out of the room with Bast scampering after her.

Chuckling to herself, Deegie returned to her preparations with a renewed zest, and after a while, she opened the kitchen curtains again. She saw nothing out of place. The pine trees all stood in their disorderly ranks, wearing their overcoats of snow, and from somewhere in their sheltering branches, a single pine grosbeak serenaded her with its call of *tee-tee too!* The awakening sun shoved the clouds aside and made diamonds on the snow, and whatever had been slinking furtively down the hill was gone now.

While the turkey roasted and filled the old house with its delectable aroma, Deegie peeled potatoes, chopped onions, whipped cream, and made several quarts of honey mead, a festive spiced drink dating back centuries. The recipe was one of the few things she had that had been given to her by her mother, and she only made it on special occasions.

Muffled thumps and the sound of dainty running paws drifted down from the second floor, and Deegie smiled. Bast, Lisbet, and the ghost cats were at it again, chasing each other around and having a grand time of it, by the sound of things. Maybe this would be the day when Lisbet felt brave enough to meet her friends, but even if she didn't, today would bring more joy and happiness than this old house had seen in decades.

* * *

Zach checked his watch for the third time in ten minutes, then got up to deliver an aggressive tap to the bathroom door. "Hey! What the hell are you doing in there, shaving your legs? Come on, man! By the time you're ready to go, it won't even be Thanksgiving anymore!"

"Unlike you, I happen to give a damn about nose hair grooming!" Gilbert swung the door open and glared at his brother while he buttoned his new white dress shirt. "Besides, it's rude to show up too early." He went into the kitchen and took an elaborate gift basket from the pantry, then began straightening the cellophane and fussing with the ribbons.

"What the *hell* is that?" Zach cocked an eyebrow at the collection of fruit and water crackers and tiny jars of jams and jellies.

"It's a gift basket for Deegie, of course. You don't go to someone's house for a meal without bringing a gift. Jeez, you really *are* a Neanderthal, aren't you?"

Zach looked down at his perfectly presentable plaid flannel shirt. "Deeg said it was nothing fancy, but whatever. Come on, let's go, ya dandy."

The Altman brothers continued to snipe at each other during the drive to Deegie's house, but their ribbing was good-natured, and they were both anxious to see their friend again. As they turned onto Fox Lane, an enormous animal with black, shaggy fur dashed out in front of the Jeep, and Zach stamped on the brake pedal with both feet. The Jeep's back end fishtailed, threatening to go into a spin, and Zach struggled grimly with the wheel as he fought for control. They ended on the side of the icy road, facing the opposite direction from which they had been heading. The dark creature continued on to the other side of the road, running through the snow in long, graceful strides.

"Holy shit!" Gilbert gasped from the passenger's seat. "What in the hell was that thing?"

Zach loosened his death grip on the steering wheel; his heartbeat thundered in his ears. "A wolf," he said. "The biggest damn wolf I've ever seen."

"What?" Gilbert stared incredulously at his brother. "There are hardly any wolves around here anymore. None that size, anyway."

"Well, I guess that one didn't get the memo. Whoo! Scared the crap out of me!" Zach restarted the stalled engine and turned the Jeep around. "Did you see the size of that thing? I thought it was a bear at first!"

"Yeah, I saw." Gilbert's breathing returned to normal, and he dried his damp palms on his neatly pressed dress slacks. As they continued up the street to Deegie's place, he kept his eyes trained on the thick forest on his right. He supposed the creature that had vanished into those trees could have been a wolf, but he had no idea they could grow so large, and the few wolves that were left in Washington State were grey, not black. As they turned into Deegie's driveway, he put the matter out of his mind; whatever that animal was, it was long gone now.

* * *

"It's still crooked." Gilbert swallowed the last of his honey mead and waggled a finger. "A little to the right."

Deegie climbed down from her stepladder perch and studied the glittery gold star she'd just placed atop a fully decked-out Christmas tree. "No it isn't! That star is perfectly straight, you jerk!" She laughed and threw a balled-up cash register receipt at him. "And you guys are supposed to be stringing that popcorn, not eating it."

Zach looked down at the half-empty bowl in his lap and guiltily brushed bits of popcorn out of his beard. "Oh yeah. I'll make more."

Deegie heaved an exaggerated sigh. "You guys!" She flapped her arms, feigning utter hopelessness, but the twinkle in her ice-blue eyes revealed her true feelings. She picked up a home décor magazine from the coffee table and studied the photos again. She had emulated the Christmas décor ideas with considerable success and her face glowed with a sense of accomplishment. "This looks about right, I think."

It was more than right; it was perfect. After they had finished their Thanksgiving dinner, Deegie had abandoned the dirty dishes in the sink and led the Altman brothers into the living room, and they watched as she created a Christmas wonderland. The six-foot tall tree, its boughs heavy with bright baubles, emitted the wonderful aroma of a pine forest. Deegie had painstakingly wound more pine boughs around a wire frame to create an equally festive wreath which hung, festooned with red ribbons, above the fireplace. On the mantle she'd placed a cut crystal bowl filled with spicy potpourri and surrounded with red, white, and green scented candles. Garlands of silver and gold tinsel were draped around the windows, framing perfectly the snow-covered landscape outside. Although the calendar claimed it was only late November, Christmas was alive and well in Deegie's house, and the early seasonal cheer belied the extraordinary horror that once lay inside.

"She thinks she's Martha Stewart," Zach whispered to his brother with a mischievous grin.

"I heard that!" She crouched beside the tree, ready to plug its connected strands of twinkle lights into a wall socket. "You guys ready? One...two...three!"

In went the plug, and the tree lit up with a constellation of multi-colored stars that competed for brilliance with the merry fire in the fireplace. Deegie clasped her hands under her chin and laughed like a child. "Look!" she exclaimed. "I made Christmas!"

"So you did! Looks gorgeous, Deeg, it really does. You did a great job." Gilbert said with obvious wonder. "It's hard to believe you've done all this as a thank-you gift for a ghost."

"So that's what Christmas looks like," said Zach. "Mom and Dad let me have a little Charlie Brown tree in my room when I was a kid, but we never had anything like this."

"Yeah, ol' Mr. Normal One had to have his Christmas tree." Gilbert landed a playful punch on his older brother's shoulder, then pointed upwards, towards the second floor. "Do you think she'll come down?"

"Maybe," Deegie said. "If I can convince her that you guys aren't going to hurt her, that is. I'll try. She needs to see this; she will love it." Stepping lightly to the foot of the wide staircase, she called out softly to the ghostly cat lady. "Lisbet? You up there, my friend? Come on down, I have a surprise for you."

Lisbet did not reply, but Deegie knew she heard. "Remember what I said I'd do if you told me where the bad men hid the book? I kept my promise, Lisbet. Please come down. I have such a surprise for you."

Something did come down the stairs then, but it wasn't Lisbet. Bast came skittering down from the second floor where he'd been playing all morning. His tiny paws were dusty, and a strand of cobweb hung from his tail. When he caught sight of the tree and its dangling ornaments, he froze on the bottom step, his golden eyes huge with wonder. Deegie scooped him up before he could pounce.

"Oh no you don't," she told the kitten. "I know what you're thinking, and you may *not* climb the tree." She brushed the dust from his fur and kissed the top of his little round head. "Where's Lisbet, huh? Have you seen her? Is she up there?"

She pretended not to notice the way Zach was gazing at her. A few weeks had passed since the supernatural battle at the end of the hall, and although Deegie had recovered physically, she still ached over the loss of Tiger Spirit. Her heart was full of pain; there wasn't room for anything else right now. A sideways glance at Gilbert caught her off guard; he was staring at her too. Feeling more than a little uncomfortable, Deegie left the room with Bast, telling the brothers that she needed to check on something in the kitchen. She stopped in the hallway, a short distance from the living room, and eavesdropped on the brothers' conversation.

"What are *you* lookin' at, douchebag?" She heard Zach mutter under his breath.

"Same thing you're looking at," was Gilbert's reply. "Give it up, Zach. She's out of your league." There was more to their conversation, but Deegie didn't want to hear it right now. She'd made good on her promise to Lisbet, and she wanted her to see the results. Holding Bast in her arms, she climbed halfway up the stairs, calling softly to her ghostly friend. "Lisbet, everything's okay now. Come on down and see what we did for you."

"Bad men..." Lisbet whispered at last.

"No, the bad men are gone. These are good men down here. They're my friends and they want to meet you."

Bast mewed in Deegie's arms, perhaps in agreement with her, or calling out to his ghostly feline playmates.

At the top of the stairs, something moved: a wispy ball of grey, like a puff of wood smoke tossed by a gentle breeze. Several more appeared, in varying shapes and sizes, all of them tumbling and rolling and twining around each other. Long tails appeared, then disappeared, and Deegie caught brief glimpses of pointed ears and bristly whiskers, dainty padded paws and glowing green eyes full of ghostly mischief.

Bast mewed again, and his shadowy playmates heeded his call. Down the stairs they came, flickering in and out of view and replying to Bast with whispery mews and faint purrs.

"Hello kitties!" Deegie greeted them, delighted by their unexpected visit. She put Bast down. "Want to play with your buddies? Go on then." The energetic kitten scrambled across the floor, his paws slipping and sliding on the polished wood, and he dove into the mass of fluffy, purring spirit energy.

Maybe Lisbet will come down later, Deegie thought, *after the guys leave. Can't really blame the poor lady; she hasn't had the best of luck with men.*

From the living room came a delicate, jingling crash: the unmistakable sound of a Christmas tree ornament hitting the floor, then the voices of both Altman brothers, calling her at once.

"Deegie! What the hell..."

"Deeg! Come in here! Check this out!"

Bast must be in the tree, she thought. *That little stinker.* She hurried back to the living room to survey the damage.

She made it to the doorway, then stood and laughed in amazement at what she saw. Her carefully decorated tree was shimmying furiously. More ornaments fell to their doom. A pair of plastic turtledoves were dislodged from the upper branches and went skidding erratically across the floor, as if propelled by playful paws. Bast sat on the coffee table watching the activities, and he offered an innocent mew, as if to say, *It wasn't me!*

"Lisbet's cats are in the tree! Bad kitties! Bad!" Deegie ran to the rapidly deconstructing tree and caught it just as it began toppling over. But her laughter belied her cross words, and she called up to the second floor again. "Lisbet! Your kitties are being very naughty! Better come see!"

"Kitty, kitty..." The voice of the ghostly cat lady drifted down the stairs.

"They're all down here, Lisbet! Come see what they did!"

Zach gasped then, pointing to the doorway. "Look!" he whispered.

Deegie spun around, following the direction of his finger. A gauzy shape, roughly the size of a small woman, wavered in and out of focus, then fully manifested. Lisbet stood in the doorway, peering shyly at the men. One hand was tucked deep into the folds of her apron, as always, and the other was pressed to her lips, holding back giggles.

"Oh, kitties, look!" said Lisbet. *"Christmas! We're home!"*

* * *

Warm, golden light spilled from the windows of the old house and made orderly, mullioned patterns on the snow outside. From inside came the sounds of muffled laughter, and a billow of smoke rose from the chimney as someone put another log on the fire. The silhouette of the woman who lived there passed in front of the window again, but the watcher in the woods was flat on his belly in the cold snow; there was no way she could see him. It was good to know she was still alive—for now. His lambent crimson eyes roamed over the festive house once more, then he rose up on his four legs, shook the snow out of his shaggy black fur, and slunk back to the sheltering woods.

EPILOGUE

ROLAND TIBBS TOSSED THE CAT o' nine tails into a corner and massaged his sore shoulder, grimacing as he did so. The two imps he'd been assigned to several weeks ago never seemed to learn from their mistakes. He didn't mind doling out punishment, and in fact rather enjoyed it, but this constant flogging of the misbehaving imps was killing his arthritic shoulder.

His two charges, Abul and Saarnu, cowered against the wall, mewling incessant apologies while their shredded flesh regenerated, ready to be flailed again. They still called one another by their human names, Johnathan and Edwin, despite strict rules against using earthly names. Roland himself had been renamed Klaa when he'd been sent to the Underworld as punishment for practicing black magic during his human life. He still thought of himself as Roland Tibbs, but he kept that to himself.

"I simply cannot believe that you two *still* don't get it!" Roland raged at the two imps. "You've both been here longer than I have, and *I* know we don't use our earthly plane names here! Why can't *you* two clowns figure it out?"

The imps bore no resemblance to the human men they had once been. Their bodies resembled lumps of clay the color of boiled lobsters, and their limbs had been shortened to barely usable stubs. Their mouths were huge and frog-like, with thick, maroon lips that looked like glistening strips of liver. This was standard procedure for new arrivals. Everyone sent to the Underworld after death started their afterlife with a new body and a new name. With good behavior, human form could be restored, albeit with some modifications. Thus, an elder demon, one who has worked hard and obeyed the laws of the Underworld, would look very much like an ordinary human, but with glowing crimson eyes and serrated, knife-like teeth. Abul and Saarnu, formerly Edwin and Johnathan Baylock, had arrived in the Underworld almost ninety years ago, but were still trapped in their imp bodies due to their ineptitude and stubbornness.

"You'll be imps for all eternity," Roland snarled disgustedly. "But if you're stupid enough to raise Chul and then *disrespect* him like you did, then I suppose you deserve it."

He opened the door to the punishment room and jabbed a finger at the vast warren of smoke and flames that lay beyond. "Get your asses out of here," he said. "I'm sure I'll be seeing you again soon."

The erstwhile Edwin and Johnathan barreled for the door, squealing, snorting, and falling over each other in their haste to get away from their whip-wielding master.

Relishing his few minutes of solitude, Roland rubbed his sore shoulder, flexed his whip arm, and wished he'd never been promoted to General of the Underworld. It was better than his last position as Chief Fire Tender, and he got to put the hurt on the rule breakers, but dealing with idiots like Abul and Saarnu was never one of his strong points.

The two-way radio on his belt crackled into life: "Sir! We have trouble in Sector Eight! We just had an open portal alert, sir!"

Open portal alerts were rare, but they were usually minor situations. Occasionally earth-plane witches, mostly inexperienced ones, would succeed in creating an opening to the Underworld, but it was generally nothing to worry about. The portals they created were usually weak, and most of them collapsed and disappeared by themselves. It took a powerful witch, like Roland himself had once been in his human life, to actually summon one of the demons that dwelled within. Roland snatched the irritating instrument from his belt. More idiots to contend with, it seemed. "Can't the Gate Keepers tend to that? That *is* their job, after all!"

"Negative, sir! The Gate Keeper's been disabled, and there's something coming through. I can't tell what it is. It's huge, and— you'd better get down here, sir!"

A cacophony of static-filled shrieks and roars came through the speaker of Roland's radio, then the communication was lost.

"Shit!" Roland shoved the radio back on his belt clip and slammed his fist against the alarm button on the wall. Alarms bellowed across the complex. An intercom was next to the alarm button, and Roland activated it with a stab of his finger, then broadcast his orders:

"All personnel to Sector Eight! Portal emergency in Sector Eight! All personnel respond immediately!"

Roland raced down the corridor, one hand holding his round-brimmed hat to his head as he ran. When he turned into the first corridor of Sector Eight, the first thing he saw was a Gate Keeper, a massive skeletal hand and arm, dragging itself to safety with what remained of its fingers. A gigantic hole yawned open in the wall, its edges aflame, and Roland caught a glimpse of another hallway, one on the Earth plane. He saw part of a kitchen, a stove, rose print wallpaper, and a young, dark-haired woman lying on the floor. Something huge and black blotted out the scene, then crossed the threshold and burst through in a billow of dark smoke and foul stench. Roland immediately recognized the paddle-like vestigial legs and the crescent, ever-grinning mouth of Chul, the demon who had been imprisoned by the very imbeciles he'd just given a sound thrashing to. He recognized what came through the portal next as well: the fully manifested form of Tiger Spirit, the Guardian Animal he'd conjured for his daughter on the night she was born.

Chul and Tiger Spirit rolled across the floor in a shower of sparks, ripping and tearing at one another and knocking demons and soldiers off their feet. Their combined battle cries were louder than the klaxon alarm that echoed throughout the Underworld. Chul sheared away and braced himself against one of the massive boulders that lined the corridor, while the missing chunks of his body regenerated. Tiger Spirit roared out his victory and, rearing up on his hind legs, spun around and leaped for the portal.

From the other side, in that earth-plane hallway, the voice of the dark-haired woman screamed out the words that would close off the rift between the two worlds: *"CLAUDERE PORTA A MALUS!"*

Roland dove for the portal too, calling out to the woman on the other side, "Deegie, no! Wait!"

He collided with the wall as the portal closed to a pinpoint, then disappeared altogether. Tiger Spirit's deadly claws raked a furrow down the wall where the portal had been, and he fell to the floor alongside Roland.

Now trapped where he didn't belong, Tiger dematerialized except for his phosphorescent eyes. His blazing yellow orbs stared hard at Roland; although this man had conjured him from the Spirit World to watch over his daughter, this was not his place, not his world. The mighty Tiger Spirit spun away, plowed through the assembly of demon soldiers, and fled down the nearest corridor. Roland followed him through the complicated maze of hallways and tunnels, and although he knew Tiger didn't speak, he yelled out, "Where is she? What happened to my daughter?"

To Be Continued...

DEEGIE'S RECIPES

IN THIS BOOK, THE CHARACTER Deegie Tibbs has an extensive knowledge of herbs and essential oils. This has also been an interest of mine for several years, and I thought it would be fun to share a few of Deegie's recipes with you. Sorry, I won't tell you how to turn someone into a frog, though. You'll have to figure that one out for yourself. Enjoy!

Broken Heart Oil

This is the recipe Deegie used after her breakup with Spencer. It has a comforting floral aroma, and the essential oils in it are known for their calming and soothing effects. Use this recipe after a bad breakup, or anytime you want to feel soothed and comforted.

1 oz. almond, jojoba, or sesame oil
6 to 12 drops rose oil blend, or 2 to 3 drops rose otto or rose absolute (see note below)
6 to 12 drops lavender essential oil
2 to 6 drops of clary sage essential oil

Mix together in a small bottle and store away from light. Start with the smaller amount of essential oil and adjust according to your preference. Find a quiet place where you can relax, and rub a few drops onto your wrists and at the base of your throat as needed. Breathe deeply and take in the beautiful scent. Especially good at bedtime as lavender helps promote restful sleep, something that is very important when dealing with wounded feelings.

A few words about essential oils: Essential oils are the liquids distilled from the leaves, flowers, stems, and other parts of plants.

They are highly concentrated, and must never be applied to the skin without diluting them. The oils most commonly used for dilution—also known as carrier oils—are almond, jojoba, and coconut oils. I prefer jojoba oil for my essential oil blends because it has a longer shelf life and does not clog pores. Rose oil blend (rose otto, and rose absolute) is sold already diluted, which saves you money due to the high cost of rose oil. I do not recommend synthetic rose oils; the scent is nowhere near as wonderful as the real thing. Essential oils can be purchased at health food stores, online, and in some drugstores. Never take any essential oil internally.

Lavender, Chamomile, and Catnip Chill-Out Tea

Did you know that catnip isn't just for our feline friends? I can imagine Deegie brewing up a nice mug of this herbal tea after a busy day at The Silent Cat, and I'm sure she'd share a bit of the catnip with little Bast!

2 teaspoons chamomile buds or the contents of a chamomile teabag
¼ teaspoon dried lavender buds
½ teaspoon dried catnip

Put the herbs into a mug, or use a metal tea ball. Pour 8 oz. of boiling water over the herbs and let the tea steep, covered, for five minutes. Strain it through cheesecloth—if you haven't used a tea ball—and sweeten to taste with honey, if desired.

Important: Pregnant women should not use catnip due to its tendency to stimulate menstruation. Fortunately, this tea tastes just as good without it!

A JAR OF FINGERS

Honey Mead (non-alcoholic version)

Deegie prepares this spicy, sweet, delicious drink for Zach and
Gilbert when they come to her house for Thanksgiving. It can be
served hot or cold, and lemon or orange slices can be added for
garnish and extra flavor.

1 quart water
1 cup honey (raw organic honey is best, but any honey will do)
¾ cup fresh-squeezed lemon juice
¼ teaspoon ground cloves
¼ teaspoon cinnamon
Pinch of nutmeg
Pinch of salt

Boil water, honey, and ½ cup of lemon juice in an enamel or glass
pot until it is reduced to 3 cups. Add the rest of the lemon juice,
spices, and salt. Shake or stir before serving.

DEEGIE'S NATURAL HAIR RINSES

DEEGIE DISCOVERED A LOT OF interesting things in the overgrown backyard of her house and among them were blackberry bushes. The leaves of the blackberry bush can be used to make an after-shampoo rinse for dark hair. It will gently enhance your hair color and adds shine and body without damage. Added color is not permanent and will wash out. I have included recipes for blondes and redheads too!

Blackberry and Black Tea Hair Rinse
for Dark Hair

½ cup of dried blackberry leaves or 100% blackberry leaf tea
3 tablespoons black tea
3 or 4 whole blackberries (optional, adds additional color)
3½ cups of water

Bring water to a boil and add all ingredients. Turn heat to low, then let simmer for about 15 minutes, then let the mixture cool and strain it. After shampooing and conditioning, pour the mixture through your hair and leave it on for 5 to 10 minutes. Rinse lightly with cool water.

Chamomile and Calendula Hair Rinse
for Blonde Hair

½ cup of dried chamomile buds or chamomile tea
3 tablespoons of dried calendula
3 tablespoons of fresh lemon juice (see note)
3 ½ cups water

Bring water to a boil, then add all ingredients. Turn heat to low, and simmer for about 10 minutes, then let cool and strain. Shampoo and condition, then pour the mixture through your hair and leave it on for 5 to 10 minutes. Rinse lightly with cool water.

Note: Although lemon juice can brighten blonde hair, it has a tendency to be drying. If your blonde locks come from a bottle, you might want to omit the lemon juice.

Raspberry, Hibiscus, and Rooibos Tea Hair Rinse
for Red and Auburn Hair

3 dried hibiscus flowers
½ cup rooibos tea
4 or 5 whole raspberries (optional, for added color)
3 ½ cups water

Bring water to a boil and add all ingredients. Turn heat to low, then simmer for 10 minutes. Let the mixture cool, then strain. After shampooing and conditioning, pour the mixture through your hair, and leave it in for 5 to 10 minutes. Rinse lightly with cool water.

Rosemary Hair Tonic
for All Hair Types and Colors

4 tablespoons fresh or dried rosemary
3 cups water
2 drops rosemary essential oil (optional)

Bring water to a boil and add rosemary. If you are using the rosemary essential oil, do not add it at this time. Turn heat to low and let simmer for 10 minutes. Let it cool, then strain it. Add the rosemary essential oil if you're using it. Shampoo, condition, then pour the mixture through your hair and massage it into your scalp. Let it sit for a few minutes, then rinse. This will stimulate blood flow to the scalp, and that helps to promote hair growth. It also helps improve dandruff and other scalp conditions.

Tips for using herbal hair rinses:

Use a condiment bottle—those yellow and red ketchup and mustard squeeze bottles—for applying your hair rinse.

After it's cool, you can add a tablespoon of apple cider vinegar to your hair rinse to help remove styling product buildup and clean your scalp.

For added fragrance, you can add 10 to 15 drops of your favorite essential oil to your hair rinse. Don't use the vinegar if you use this option, though. The vinegar smell doesn't mix well with the essential oils.

Keep any leftover hair rinse in the fridge and use within a week.

ABOUT THE AUTHOR

C.L. HERNANDEZ IS AN AUTHOR of fiction, horror, and dark fantasy. She has been writing since she was very young, but never gave a thought to being published until 2012. In 2014, she self-published two short story collections, *Cobwebs* and *A Half-Dozen Horrors*, and a short, true-life ghost story called *A Woman's Touch*. In addition to writing, she enjoys crocheting and a variety of crafts. She lives in California's Central Valley with her daughter, Olivia, two cats, and a turtle named George.

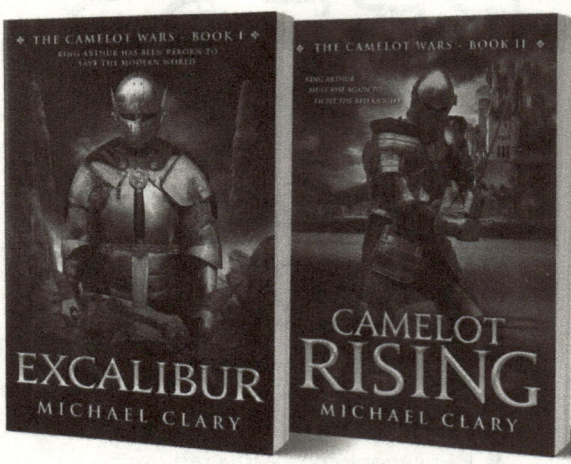

THE ULTIMATE PREPPER'S ADVENTURE.
THE JOURNEY BEGINS HERE!

EAN 9781682611654 $9.99   EAN 9781618687371 $9.99   EAN 9781618687395 $9.99

The long-predicted Coronal Mass Ejection has finally hit the Earth, virtually destroying civilization. Nathan Owens has been prepping for a disaster like this for years, but now he's a thousand miles away from his family and his refuge. He'll have to employ all his hard-won survivalist skills to save his current community, before he begins his long journey through doomsday to get back home.

PERMUTED
PRESS

THE MORNINGSTAR STRAIN HAS BEEN LET LOOSE—IS THERE ANY WAY TO STOP IT?

EAN 9781618686497 $16.00

An industrial accident unleashes some of the Morningstar Strain. The doctor who discovered the strain and her assistant will have to fight their way through Sprinters and Shamblers to save themselves, the vaccine, and the base. Then they discover that it wasn't an accident at all—somebody inside the facility did it on purpose. The war with the RSA and the infected is far from over.

This is the fourth book in Z.A. Recht's The Morningstar Strain series, written by Brad Munson.

PERMUTED
PRESS

GATHERED TOGETHER AT LAST, THREE TALES OF FANTASY CENTERING AROUND THE MYSTERIOUS CITY OF SHADOWS...ALSO KNOWN AS CHICAGO.

From *The New York Times* and *USA Today* bestselling author Richard A. Knaak comes three tales from Chicago, the City of Shadows. Enter the world of the Grey—the creatures that live at the edge of our imagination and seek to be real. Follow the quest of a wizard seeking escape from the centuries-long haunting of a gargoyle. Behold the coming of the end of the world as the Dutchman arrives.

Enter the City of Shadows.

PERMUTED
PRESS